# Goat Tales

## The Izzy Journals!

# Goat Tales

## The Izzy Journals!

By Izzy 1982 -1993

Edited by Tacy Thurn Ellis
Illustrations by Don Collins

# bright sky press

Box 416, Albany, Texas 76430

10  9  8  7  6  5  4  3  2  1

Library of Congress Cataloging-in-Publication Data

Ellis, Tacy Thurn.
Goat tales : the Izzy journals: 1982-1993 / by Tacy Thurn Ellis ; illustrated by
Don Collins. p. cm.

Summary: Despite some silly misunderstandings when she first arrives, Izzy soon
becomes a family favorite and a leader among the animals on a north central
Texas farm. Includes glossary and facts and historical information about goats.

ISBN-13: 978-1-931721-78-3 (cloth : alk. paper) 1. Goats-juvenile fiction. [1.
Goats-Fiction. 2. Domestic animals-Fiction. 3. Farm life-Texas-Fiction. 4.
Texas-Fiction.] I. Collins, Don, ill. II. Title.

PZ10.3.E5476Goa 2006
[Fic]-dc22                                                          2006011731

Book and cover design by Dwain Kelley and Mary Barminski Johnson
of Kelleygraphics, Austin, Texas

*Printed and bound in China by Sun Fung Offset Binding Co. Ltd.*

*The characters in this book are real.
The names have not been changed because
no one is completely innocent.*

# TABLE OF CONTENTS

## Part I - The First Day

## Part II - The Rest of My Life

# PART ONE

*Today is the first day of the rest of your life*
– Charles Dederich

## 1. HOME

I knew I was smaller than all of the other kids. People kept reaching over the fence for them and handing the man paper from their pockets. The others didn't come back. By the third day, a Sunday, at First Monday Trade Days, I was the only one left, so I looked pretty big all alone in the pen. It was later that day when my life changed.

"She's all skin and bones," remarked a tall, two-legged kid. The man with him agreed. They were peering over the fence at me and shaking their

heads from side to side. I stood and stretched to shake the sleep from my body.

"We really don't need another animal," the tall man said.

"I'll help take care of her while I stay with you," said the kid.

"Oh, if we took her home, she'd be taken care of...my wife would see to that. How much?"

The man who had brought me to the trade day began to haggle with the tall man. I went to the fence beside the two-legged kid. He reached over and lifted me into his arms. I pitched my head back to see his face, and when I did, I hit his chin with my horn button. "Ow! You're feisty for a skinny one!" exclaimed the kid. "Is he gonna come down?" he asked the tall man. "Is he?"

"Is that what you're gonna call her?" the tall man asked the kid.

"What?"

"Izzy?"

"Izzy? Sure! If she's going with us!" the kid answered.

"Well, if that's what you want to spend your ten dollars on, James, then she's yours."

"Cool! Aunt Tacy will love her!"

They made the paper trade with the man, and we walked away. James was carrying me. My head was over his shoulder. I watched the man by the empty fenced lot count his green paper.

It was a long trip home. James and the tall man argued at first about where I should ride. The tall man said they could tie my feet and put me in the back of the truck. But James argued that I was too small and skinny and that the wind might blow me out. I didn't think I would blow out, but I was glad for the argument, because it got me a ride inside the truck on James's lap. I was a little restless; I chewed the radio dial, and the gearshift, and the glove box, and the buttons on James's shirt, and his ear. (I was a little hungry, too.) I finally decided James's lap was the softest place to be, so I plopped down on it, and with a wriggle of my tail and tuck of my head, I was asleep.

I awoke as the ride ended – because I nearly bounced out of the truck as it entered the driveway! James was stretching his neck over the dashboard, looking for someone. "Do you see her, Uncle Mark?"

"Nope," responded the tall man, as he continued to hit every hole in the driveway.

"She'll like Izzy. I know she will."

"Yep," the tall man agreed, as the truck came to a stop.

We got out of the truck, and James put me on the ground. It was great! I stretched and jumped and smelled the grass. Then I looked around. It had only been a couple of seconds, but the guys were gone! I looked everywhere. Finally, after about fifteen seconds of bleating at the top of my lungs, I heard a slam and turned to the sound. Whew! There they were. They had come out of a house and onto a porch. "Shhhhhhhhh," they said to me. They were making sounds like a rattlesnake I heard once, and I couldn't imagine why! I ran to James.

"Izzy," he said, "If you want to stay here, you'll have to be quieter." He laughed and rubbed my horn buttons. "Here she comes."

James pointed to a two-legged figure walking up from a barn. All I could do was watch. As it got closer, I noticed it was a little different from the guys. It had longer hair. I watched it walk and listened to it greet the guys. "Hi, Mark. Hi, James. Did you have a good time?" The voice was different. I hid behind James's leg, hoping to go unnoticed.

"Aunt Tacy, we got you something."

"Correction: James got you something," said the tall man.

"Uh-oh...what did you do?" the figure asked gently, as it knelt down beside me and peeped around James's leg.

I looked up and met its eyes. That's when I realized it was a girl, like me! Her smell was different. She smiled differently. She put her hands on either side of my face and rubbed my eyes with her thumbs. "Is it staying?" she asked.

"If you want her to," said James. "I bought her for you. Her name's Izzy."

"Izzy." She looked at me, right into my eyes. I knew I had a home.

"MAAAAA!" I said. "MAAAAA!" I jumped sideways, twisting my body and running at the same time. (That's one of my favorite ways to play.) They all laughed, so I did it again, this time in the other direction, and they laughed again. Life was good!

*...She was one of those happily creative beings who please without effort, make friends everywhere, and take life so gracefully and easily, that less fortunate souls are tempted to believe that such are born under a lucky star.*
– Louisa May Alcott

## 2 . THE BEAST

It was on my fourth or fifth gallivant when I hit her. She came out of nowhere! We hit against each other's sides, and I fell to my knees. I looked up to see a terribly long nose looking down at me. It was cold on the tip, and it kept sniffing me. It went into my ears and sniffed, and a long tongue came out just below it and licked my mouth and nose. I thought it would smother me, and I panicked! I tried to get up too fast, and my legs shot out from under me in four different directions. I was scrambling as fast as my little cloven hooves could! The nose was still right there, only now it was pushing me and licking my tail. I finally made it to my feet and ran away, as far as I could. Then, while I was running, I realized that I needed to be brave and protect my new Tacy from the beast. I stopped and turned abruptly, reared up on my hind legs, and bent my head down to challenge the thing. That's when I got my first look at the whole beast.

It was about five times bigger than I was, and it had hair all over its body! It was black with white feet and white on its tail. Its tail was waving wildly back and forth from side to side. Its whole body swayed, starting with the tail and all the way to its shiny wet nose, which hovered right above its shiny white teeth and its long, pink, dangling tongue. I knew that I would soon be eaten! Then I heard the laughter from the members of the gang, who were still just sitting in the grass. I couldn't believe it! Here I was, battling the fiercest beast on earth – and had been doing so for at least thirty or forty seconds – while there they were, lounging in the grass, laughing!

"MAAAAA!" I said.

"AAARF!" the beast said, and jumped sideways, twisting its body and running at the same time.

I cocked my head to the side and considered this. I knew these motions: the beast wanted to play! "Be brave, Izzy!" I thought to myself. I gulped and then, with a loud "MAAAAAA," I jumped in the opposite direction from the beast and  stopped to see what would happen. It mirrored my actions and spoke again, and it began running wildly in circles, finally coming to rest next to my Tacy. She patted the beast and said, "It's okay, Timbra. Good dog."

"Dog?" I thought to myself. "Timbra." I approached and Timbra reached her nose to mine. Her big tongue licked my chin. I returned the favor as the gang looked on and laughed. I plopped down beside Timbra. She was warm and soft, and sleep came right away for me.

*I have learned that to have a good friend is the purest of all God's gifts, for it is a love that has no exchange of payment.* – Frances Farmer

## 3. HUNGER AND HOOF CONTROL

When I woke up (yes, I did nap a lot), Timbra had her head across my back and was breathing gently with her eyes closed. I could hear her heart beating slow and steady. I looked around. There was a fence. There was grass. There was a tree and a house, and beautiful red and yellow and pink and orange plants were all around it. They were so pretty! I wiggled. Timbra moved her head and stretched out on her side to continue sleeping. The colors around the house were calling to me; they had a smell that was sweet, and my stomach was growling. I stuck my tail and hind side in the air and stretched. Then I put my front legs under me, one at a time, and stretched again. I started for the colors.

They each had a different smell. The orange ones were the brightest, but they didn't smell very good. I gave one a little nibble...YUCK! The orange was bitter! I snorted and blew. I jumped to the next color which was inside a small rock border. I stepped all over those orange ones, because I would not want anyone ever to have to taste them. The pink ones were much sweeter and easier to tear and chew. I could almost reach some of the bright red ones and was leaning across some white ones when I lost my footing and rolled right through the yellow ones. It took a little bit of scrambling to get my feet untangled, and I trampled a few of the colors before I went back to sampling more.

"My flowers!" screamed my Tacy, and she started toward me. She was moving pretty fast and to the side a little, so I jumped to the side, twisting my body and running...right through the rest of the colors. By then she was close enough for me to see her face, and I could tell she was not happy. She stopped when she got to the rock border and knelt down, trying to stand the orange-colored plants back up. Boy, it was a confusing time for me. I just stood there and watched.

When she finally realized that I had done too good a trampling job on most of the flowers, she sat back and looked at me.

"Maaaaa?" I asked.

"All right, I know you didn't know these were my flowers. Judging by the job you've done on them, you must be pretty hungry. What do you eat, anyway?"

"Maaaaa!" I said, jumping toward her and putting my front hooves on her shoulder.

She fell back and laughed. "Izzy! Okay, okay...you are hungry! Let's see what we can find." She picked me up, tucked me under her arm, and carried me inside the house. To this day, I don't understand why people live in those things: hard, wooden, slippery floors...I just don't know. Anyway, she set me down on the slick floor in what she called the "kitchen." On the floor next to the door were some glass bottles with "Coca-Cola" in red on the side. I was so excited! I knew the taste of warm, sweet milk that came from those bottles! I started toward them, but every step I took made my legs slip out from under me! That kitchen floor was the slickest thing I had ever tried to stand on. I got my rear legs under me and then got to my front knees, but when I would try to push up one front leg...DOWN I would go again. Those bottles weren't getting any closer!

"Maaaaa!" I screamed. My Tacy turned from where she had water running and started laughing at me. Because I was exhausted, I just quit right there. I flopped my head right down on that hard wooden floor. "Ow!" I thought. "Maaaaa!" I cried.

My Tacy, still chuckling, came over and lifted me to my feet. "Try moving a little more slowly, Izzy. Then that floor won't seem nearly as hard," she suggested.

I did move more slowly, and the bottles did get closer. But they didn't smell the same as the ones I had eaten from, and the rubber thing that I needed to suckle on wasn't there. I just looked at them and then up at my Tacy. I was standing there, trying to see what she was doing with her hands on the big box in front of her, when I felt my feet begin to slide out to each side. I slid down to the ground slowly and wound up with my head stuck between two of the cola bottles.

> *It had long since come to my attention that people of accomplishment rarely sat back and let things happen to them. They went out and happened to things.*
> – Mark Twain

## 4. RINGING MAKES THE MILK TASTE BAD

"So, you know what a bottle is," said my Tacy. She went to a big white box and opened it. When she did, a cool breath of air came out of it and floated across me. She took out a jug with white liquid in it. It looked like milk to me. She poured some in the Coca-Cola bottle and then took a hand-shaped thing that smelled like rubber and cut off a finger from it. I watched with curiosity. She poked a hole in the end of the finger from that rubber hand and put it over the bottle end. She twisted this stretchy thing around it to make it stay, and then she offered it to me.

"Izzy, here's some milk. Let's see if you like it," she said. I put my nose to it and sniffed. It smelled like milk. I pulled the rubber finger with my teeth,

being careful not to touch it with my lips. When I let it go, it snapped back and milk squirted out onto my nose and into my eyes. I snorted. My Tacy laughed, so I snorted again and she laughed again. She reached over and wiped my face clean. She patted my side. She was the closest thing to my mother that I could remember.

Just then, some really loud ringing began. It was coming from a device on the wall. It wouldn't stop. My Tacy started right for the device. I had to do something! I had to save her! I started toward her feet with the best "kitchen legs" I had and darted right in front of her. Instead of stopping, she tripped over me and began falling. She tried to catch herself along the wall below the device, and her hand caught a long, curly cord, which pulled on the device. A portion of it popped off and fell right down on my Tacy, hitting her squarely on the forehead. She grabbed her head with one hand and the piece of the device with the other. "Hello?" she said, speaking into the device.

"Maaaaa," I answered.

"Hello?" she said.

"Maaaaa?" I asked.

"Izzy! Be quiet!" demanded my Tacy, in a not-so-happy tone. That's when I noticed it was quiet. I had stopped the thing from ringing! I had saved the day! Oh, sure, my Tacy had a bump on her forehead, which was turning a pretty purple color now, but I had stopped the ringing and saved her from a much worse fate.

"Hello?" she said. "Yes, I'm here. Hi Martha... Well, I have a goat...No, it's still young enough for a bottle..." My Tacy kept talking into the device while she got up and put the milk jug back in the box. The long, curly cord went with her. "I don't know. I think cow's milk is okay...I hadn't thought about it not having enough vitamins," continued my Tacy. "Do you think I should add some? I have some from the vet clinic, that you sent with me...Okay, well, she is a little skinny," she added, while looking down at me and holding a wet cloth on her forehead. She began again, "I'll add some to the milk, and she should suckle them right down...Thanks, Martha...Her name? Oh, it's Izzy." And she put the device back on the wall.

"My name," I thought. "My name...I have a name." I looked up to see her taking the rubber finger off the bottle and pouring something in. Just then, a smell struck me. It was like smelly fish. My Tacy put a lid back on a little brown bottle. Then she replaced the rubber finger and started toward me.

"Aaaaah, milk!" I thought, and grabbed the end of that rubber finger and began to suckle. It wasn't warm, but that was okay. I continued to suckle...and then it hit me: whatever had made that fishy smell was in the bottle and it was in the milk. It not only smelled like smelly fish, it tasted like I imagined they would taste! Whatever that ringing thing told her to do had spoiled my milk! "YUCK!" I thought. I spit that rubber finger out and began to spit and snort and spin and spit some more. I wondered if my Tacy was trying to poison me! I sneezed and spit again and snorted. The taste would not go away!

"It's only vitamins, Izzy. I'm sorry," apologized my Tacy.

I vowed right there that I would never suckle a bottle again! My Tacy tried to make me think she had washed the bottle and the glove, but I could still smell the fishy vitamins. I clamped my teeth down and refused even to taste the new bottle she claimed to have prepared. Every time she tried to put it in my mouth, I refused. She finally walked away in distress, wiping milk from her face, shirt, and hands.

Now, it seemed at the time like a good idea to refuse fishy milk, but later, when I was outside, my stomach began to growl loudly. I was hungry – really hungry! But I knew I couldn't trust that bottle. I longed for something, but what?

*If you harden your heart with pride,*
*you soften your brain with it, too.*
        – Jewish Proverb

# 5. RAISINS

People say that goats will eat anything. Well, they are wrong. My Tacy offered me everything, and I didn't eat any of it. I had never seen any of it before. For a long time – it must have been at least twenty minutes – I wouldn't even taste anything she offered. I would nibble on grass and a flower if I could get close enough. I think I was losing weight by the second, and I could tell that my Tacy was worried about me.

First, she offered me what she called "oats." They smelled pretty good, but they were so dry that I refused to eat any after the first one. She called something "alfalfa" and offered it to me. It was green and smelled pretty good, but it was dry, too, like the oats. She walked into the house and came out with a box. It was white with light blue on it and said "Premium Saltines" on the side. She opened a package and pulled out a small square thing that she called a "cracker." It was too dry, so I sneezed on it. She went back in and brought out another box that had a man in a blue hat and a boat on it. "How about some Captain Crunch?" my Tacy asked.

"Maaaaa," I replied, and walked away.

"Izzy, you have to eat something." She picked me up and carried me back to the big white box. "Maybe there's something in the refrigerator," she said, opening it. (That's when I learned its name.) It was very bright in the refrigerator, but my eyes focused on a bright red box. My Tacy set me down, and I stood in front of the refrigerator, enjoying the cool air and staring at the red box.

She offered me an apple, but I snorted at it. She offered me a carrot, but I snorted at that, too. I moved closer to the box and leaned toward it. I almost had it when my front feet slipped back between my rear feet. Down I went again on that slick floor, but on the way down, I latched my teeth onto a piece of that pretty red box so that it went down with me. We both hit hard on the floor, and the box spit out several little black wrinkly things.

The wrinklies didn't look very good, but as I was getting up, I sniffed one. It smelled so sweet! I pushed my lips and muzzle against it. It was soft. I nibbled on the edge, and it tasted as sweet as it smelled, so I ate it. It was wonderful! It was great! I cocked my head sideways and jumped. I fell, but it was okay, because I was next to the wrinklies. I picked another one up and ate it while I lay on my side.

"Raisins? Raisins! Of all the things in the world, Izzy, you want raisins?" asked Tacy.

"Maaaaa!" I exclaimed, and I stood up to give her a little nudge with my head. My Tacy reached into the box and pulled out a few more. I stood on my hind feet and reached for them; I grabbed one just as

I slipped and fell again. Tacy giggled. She picked me up in one hand and grabbed the raisins in the other, and we went outside.

*It's a funny thing about life: if you refuse to accept anything but the best, you very often get it.*
– Somerset Maugham

## 6. A PLACE TO REST

Back outside, Tacy let me eat raisins until I was full. She mumbled about them being expensive and wondered how many I could eat without getting sick. I tried to tell her that I could eat all of them, but she didn't seem to understand.

Once I was full, I got sleepy. I stood beside my Tacy while she sat in the grass with me. Timbra was with us, too. My eyes grew so heavy that I had to close them. My Tacy petted me while I stood there. She scratched itches I didn't know I had, and it felt so good. Hands and fingers are a good thing, almost as handy as teeth.

"My goodness, it's late. Where are we going to put you tonight?" asked Tacy. I tried to tell her that I would sleep with her, but she didn't seem to be listening. She just kept looking around. And then she spotted it: a little gray shed, down behind the house. "The chicken pen...that's it!" she exclaimed. "Izzy, you've got a place to sleep." She stood and began walking away from me. Timbra went with her. I was still very sleepy and for just a second, my head drooped and my eyes closed, and sweet visions of wrinklies...I mean, raisins...filled my head. Just then, I heard footsteps behind me!

*The lens of fear magnifies the size of the uncertainty.*
– Charles Swindoll

## 7. MONSTER!

I didn't have time to think! My head came up, and I perked my ears, and I could see my Tacy headed for the little gray building. The footsteps were nearing, and I was afraid! I dared not look back! I just started screaming "Maaaaa!" and running after my Tacy and Timbra! I don't know if it was my screaming that stopped them, but they turned and waited for me. I ran to the right and bounced a few times until my rear end passed my front end, and I went into a spin. Then I ran to the left and started bouncing, and it happened again. It's very strange: your feet just wrap up around each other, and your

tail goes right past your ears, and before you know it, you are spun to the ground. The whole world turns after that.

I glanced back behind me to see a huge monster in the yard near where I had been. I could tell it was a monster, because I had never seen one before. It was gray with a hump and long, pointy things sticking out of the side of its head. Now, goats have what we call horns, but they are on the tops, or polls, of our heads, and they grow straight back, not out to the side. And this creature was huge! It had a long tail and four legs. It stood where I had been and sniffed. It sniffed the air, the ground, the red box, and then the ground again.

I stood and looked back at it. From this distance it didn't seem as large as it had sounded. It made a low wooing sound, and Tacy hollered at it, "Charlie, you get out of my yard!" The thing, the monster, didn't move. She continued, "Charlie! I mean it! You get out of my yard!" The big monster looked in our direction. Its eyes were coal black. It stuck out its tongue and cleaned its nostrils. Finally, it turned its large, slow body and went out the gate it had come through, disappearing into the brush. I wasn't sure what it was. But, at any rate, my Tacy had made it leave.

*How rarely we weigh our neighbor in the same*
*balance in which we weigh ourselves.*
– Thomas à Kempis

## 8. THE COOP

We headed on into a fenced lot that was around the building my Tacy called "the chicken coop." It was full of weeds and dead grass. I nibbled on a little of each. I was getting hungry again, as raisins just don't go too far. Tacy went inside and began moving things around. I went to the door of the building. It was dark inside, because there was only one window on the south side of the place. The door was on the south, too. It was hazy, and dust floated everywhere because of Tacy's rustling around. There were several boxes in a row on the wall. There was an old tire in another corner with hay inside of it. There were a couple of bars hanging from the ceiling and more pipe bars in front of the wall boxes. There were two big cinder blocks on the ground that supported a couple of pieces of lumber about twelve to sixteen inches high. There were a lot of feathers!

Tacy had moved around behind me and was making her way in and out of the door with shovels full of the stuff that was on the ground. She put it in a wheelbarrow and said something about a garden. On her last trip inside, she shook several large pieces of hay into the corner. Next, she found a plastic bucket and washed it and filled it with water before putting it in the pen. "There. That should do it, Izzy. You will be very comfortable in here tonight." And with that, she shut the gate.

"Maaaaa!" I yelled as she walked away, pushing the wheelbarrow, but she didn't turn around or even stop. She just kept walking. I called to her again, but this time she was out of earshot. I had to do something! She had accidentally locked me in a lot with feathers all over it! I ran up and down the fence a couple of times, but there were no holes. I ran in the building – and out! It was dark and scary in there! I ran to the gate I had come through. I could see the latch was fastened, so I looked down...BINGO! There was a small hatch for a chicken to pass through, leading to the free world! I got down on my knees, crawled through, and ran as fast as I could to find my Tacy.

*You can't appreciate home till you've left it. –* O. Henry

## 9. GARDENING CAN BE FUN!

The sun was getting lower in the western sky. I saw my Tacy holding a long pole with a chopper on the end of it. She had emptied the wheelbarrow, and it sat beside her as she spread what had been its contents all over the ground. I was so happy to see her! I did that running thing where my hind end passed my front end, and when I went into a spin, I wound up flipping end over end and landing right at Tacy's feet. She looked down at me and asked, "How'd you get out?"

"Maaaaa," I answered, trying to explain that I understood how it could have happened that she accidentally locked me in.

"Well," she said, picking me up and brushing the dead grass from my coat, "I guess I'll have to work on that fence. We'll finish up here, and then we'll do just that."

She started chopping her pole into the ground around her plants. I stood there for a moment and watched. I noticed that I was surrounded by green plants that all had some sort of yummy-looking leaf on them. Ever so often she would pull off a leaf, pick up something she had chopped, and pitch it to the edge of her garden.

"I can help!" I thought. I pulled a leaf or two off and then walked a couple of steps closer to her. Those were tasty and she was still pulling a few, so I started in on another plant. It really had good flavor! Maybe I stayed too long at that one plant, though, because in a minute I heard a "NOOOOOO!" I turned to see my Tacy running toward me. I thought there must have been something after me, so I turned to see what it was. I didn't see anything, so I thought one more bite would be okay, but she kept running and screaming. It wasn't until she added my name into her sentences that I realized I had done something wrong and that she was chasing me!

Tacy was running and jumping sideways over

rows of plants. She was headed straight toward me. I knew that sideways move: she was playing! I turned my head and bounded sideways, too. Tacy mirrored my steps. I went the other way, and she did that, too! But then I looked into her face, and I realized that perhaps I was doing something wrong: not only had I eaten her favorite banana pepper plant, but in running sideways, I had broken off several other kinds of peppers, some tomatoes, and even two volunteer stalks of okra.

She was out of breath. She dropped to her knees and shook her head. "I worked all spring on those plants, and in one day, Izzy – one day! – you wiped out half my garden!"

I looked around. I had broken many of the plants. I felt badly about it, too. I did the only thing I knew to do. Since I hate to be wasteful, I grabbed a leaf, cocked my head to the side, and jumped sideways toward her.

My Tacy shook her head and let out an "Aughhh!" but then a smile took over her face and laughter followed. "Let's get that fence fixed," she said, starting toward the wheelbarrow. I beat her to it, rear end first, of course. So I jumped in and stood there. She lifted the wheelbarrow bars and started pushing. I did a little turn-around jig in the wheelbarrow and jumped out. I took two bounds and then turned around and jumped twice, landing back in the wheelbarrow. Tacy just laughed and kept pushing. Satisfied with my antics, I enjoyed the rest of the ride back to the chicken pen.

*Love doesn't make the world go 'round. Love is what makes the ride worthwhile. – F. P. Jones*

## 10. REINFORCEMENTS

Tacy walked up to the house to get what she called a "hammer" and a few spikes to go with it. I tagged along beside her. I was ready for more raisins by that time. (Leaps and bounds deplete the system, you know.) On the way back toward the pen, she stopped and grabbed a couple of pieces of lumber. Her arms were pretty full, but she had forgotten the raisins. I tried to remind her by getting in front of her and turning her back toward the house. I guess the lumber obscured  her view of me, for when I made my pass toward the house, her feet tangled up and in just a matter of seconds, the lumber and my Tacy were both on the ground! She really should be much more careful.

"Izzy!" she shouted. I could tell she was

concerned. She must have sensed my hunger. "Izzy! I am going to get you..."

"Maaaaa!" I cheered. Raisins! She was going to get me raisins!

She reached for me, but I couldn't wait! I took off toward the house. She righted herself and piled up the lumber she had been carrying. I turned back toward her and she grabbed at me again, but I had already started again for the house. This time she ran after me! "Yea!" I thought. "Raisins are at the house! We're running for raisins!" It was only about thirty seconds before we reached the porch where the red box was. I picked it up by one of its tabs and trotted it over to Tacy.

"Is that what all this is about, Izzy? More raisins?"

"Maaaaa!" I answered, shaking my head up and down and snorting.

"Okay, well, if you want raisins, you are going to have to eat them in your new house," said Tacy.

"Okay," I thought, and pranced up to the door on the porch.

"Oh, no. This isn't where you are staying. Your house is down with the chickens." With that, she started down to the chicken pen once again, only this time, she had the raisins. I followed willingly.

*Better bend than break.* – Scottish Proverb

# 11. YOU WANT ME TO SLEEP WHERE?

By the time we got the lumber, it was almost what some call "dusk." That is the time in the evening when the sun doesn't hurt your eyes anymore, and all the things between you and the sun look like black shadows that everyone calls "silhouettes." The chickens were coming into their house for the evening. They came in one by one, the biggest first, and jumped onto the bars in front of the wall boxes. There they sat, their heads cocked to the side, just looking me over.

Tacy had nailed lumber over the little hatch I had earlier escaped through. She patched two other holes that looked like they could be alternate routes. I watched in curiosity. Did she really think I was staying here? That I would sleep here?

Mark had come back home by then. Tacy asked him to run an extension cord down to the coop. While he was doing that, she dug out a brooding lamp from the chicken pen and hung it over some hay that she had laid in the corner. It was almost dark when they plugged it in.

When the light came on, the chickens all squawked

a little. The light shined from below them and cast big feathery shadows on the wall behind them. It was creepy! My Tacy was nuts if she thought I was sleeping here! I went and stood by the gate.

Tacy picked me up, put me on the hay under the lamp, and fed me a raisin.

I went and stood at the gate.

She picked me up again, put me back under the lamp, and put some oats in a bucket with raisins on top of them.

I went back and stood at the gate.

"Fine, Izzy, suit yourself!" she said. "But you'll be warmer in the coop." With that, she and Mark scooted out the gate and locked it in front of me. I watched for a minute while their shadows moved away toward the barn.

"MAAAAAA! MAAAAA! MAA!" I cried, but the shadows moved further away. I ran to the corners of the pen...no way out! I ran to the corners of the shed...again, no way out! I ran to the gate and put my head against it. It gave a little! I pushed a little harder, and it gave a little more. The latch was at the top, but the bottom of the gate would open just enough...for me to escape once again!

*The head learns new things, but the heart forevermore practices old experiences.* – Henry Ward Beecher

## 1 2 .  " S C A P E  G O A T "

When I got my last leg out, I looked for the shadows, but they must have reached the barn. No matter – I knew which way the house was. I started walking toward the house with pride, my head held high and my tail in the air, excited that I had out-smarted the gate. It was very scary out there, though. Shadows came at me from all directions, and it felt like things were closing in on me. Blades of tall grass rubbed on each other, and when something rustled to my left, I started running at full speed, my neck stretched straight out! Lucky for me, this time my rear end stayed behind my front end, but when I got to the porch, I couldn't stop, so I jumped from the ground to the top step – and slid right into the door!

The door was closed. There were no sounds inside. I murmured a low "maaa" in the hope that my Tacy would hear me. There was a light above me, and summer bugs flitted into it and away from it and back in again. I watched one bug as it dived down, down, down and then up, up, up. "Whoa! What was that?" I thought. No, it wasn't the bug, but something that had caught my eye when I watched the bug dive down. I turned my head

toward a window, and I saw it again!

I darted around the corner of the porch. After a long while, at least twenty or thirty seconds, I peeped around the corner. I couldn't see anything. I stayed along the porch wall and sneaked up to the window, and when I was right beside it, I popped my head around and looked in.

There it was again! I jumped back and looked again. Then, I pulled my head back slowly, and it did the same. I poked it with my nose, and it poked back...well, sort of, because it was behind the glass. I conjured up all my courage and looked at it full in its face. It just looked back. It had four legs and a little short tail. It had brown hair that was shaggy, a lot like mine; it had a white blaze on its face; it had black accent hair down its topline and around its knees and its four cloven hooves. The pupils in its eyes were not round, but sat sideways; the ears on its head didn't hang down all the way or stand up all the way; and it had two little bumps on the poll of its head.

I turned my head to one side, and it did, too. I turned my body to the side, and it turned, also. I was annoyed by now that it was copying me. I stood on my hind legs and cocked my head to warn it to go away, but it did the same thing. Finally, I just stopped and kept looking at it.

As I was standing there, I heard my Tacy talking. She was getting closer. "Oh, Mark, she just looked and sounded so helpless down there."

"She'll be fine."

"You don't think the coyotes or an owl will get her, do you, Mark?"

"No, nothing will get her. That fence won't let anything in."

"But it let me out," I thought as they rounded the corner of the house.

"Will you look at that! The little scamp!"

exclaimed Tacy.

"Well, how'd you do that, little goat? Are you a 'scape goat'?" Mark asked as he picked me up and chuckled. I tried to tell him, but he just kept saying to me, "Easy, girl" and "Quiet, now." I tried to explain about the dark and the shadows, and then I started asking about the thing in their window, but neither of them understood. Mark set me down again, saying, "I'll take her back down there."

"No, I can do it. I'll sit with her until she sleeps," Tacy insisted. Sleep. Now that was beginning to sound really good.

"Come on, Izzy," Tacy said, and started down toward the chicken coop.

"Go on," said Mark, and he gave me a little push.

"Izzy, come on," Tacy called. Mark had gone inside by now and Tacy was nearing the shadows. I ran to catch up to her before I was left all alone.

*We pardon to the extent that we love.*
– Francois de La Rochefoucauld


## 13. SLEEP TIGHT

I ran as fast as I could, and when I caught her, I darted right in front of her. She tripped and began falling. I tried to catch her, but her feet got even more tangled. Finally, she wound up on the ground. I put my feet on her chest and looked down into her face. I could see pretty well, because that big, round nightlight was hanging in the sky. She put her hands on either side of my face and stroked my eyes like she had earlier in the day. She looked right at me and asked, "What am I going to do with you, Izzy?" Then she sat up and pulled me in and gave me a big hug. Stumbling to her feet, she carried me to the chicken coop.

She was confused when she got to the gate, as it was still latched. She unlatched it and held me while she kicked all around the bottom of the fence to find where I had gotten out. When she got back to the gate, she kicked the hatch, and when the bottom of the gate gave, she figured it out. "Well, I can fix that when I go. Izzy, I am going to leave you here tonight...and you, Izzy, are going to stay where I put you." Her voice was lulling me to sleep. I was so tired. It had been such a wonderful, adventurous, exciting, long day. My head was spinning, and I really was getting sleepy.

Tacy stepped to the corner and sat down. She held me to her chest. I looked up at her eyes, and she offered me a raisin. I ate it, and she offered another, but I was too tired. My ear was bent back against her, and I could hear a heartbeat. It was a little slower than the one I remembered from before the man took me to the trade day, but it was strong and steady, and it drummed me to sleep. I remember looking up to make sure she was still holding me, and she was right there. I vaguely remember being placed in the hay, under the brood lamp. It was so warm, and sleep came so easily....

"Today was the first day of the rest of my life," I thought. "I wonder what tomorrow will bring?" I remember peeping through heavy eyelids at two feet leaving the barn. However, I was too tired, too warm, and too happy to care.

*And isn't it, my boy or girl, the wisest, bravest plan,*
*whatever comes, or doesn't come, to do the best you can.*
– Phoebe Cary

# PART TWO

*The scenes of childhood are the memories of future years.* – The Farmer's Almanack, 1850

## 14. ROOSTER C.

The first morning, and every morning after that for several years, I woke up to the sound of Rooster C. He was red with a furry face and big, gray legs with short, sharp spurs on them. "ER-ER-ER-ER-ERRR!" he crowed. I just about came out of my skin! I jumped up and bumped my head on the brood lamp and then turned too fast and ran into the wall. I shook my head and looked around. Rooster C. was still on his roost in front of the wall boxes. He was stretching his leg out behind him and flapping his wings, sending dust everywhere. The other chickens were beginning to do the same, but instead of crowing, they were clucking softly.

It was gray and damp outside, for there was no sunlight yet. I heard my stomach growl. I remembered that there were raisins somewhere, and looking around I saw two buckets. I moved to the first one and stuck my nose in to sniff for the luscious fruits. I nearly drowned! It was full of water instead of raisins. I snorted and blew and shook my head. I stuck my head in the other bucket, cautiously. There was the wonderful smell of those little black wrinklies! They were scattered on the oats just like Tacy had left them the night before. I gobbled them up as quickly as I could, and I even nibbled at the oats beneath them.

I was standing there nibbling, my head in the bucket, when my ears broke! Right next to me, Rooster C. launched one of his "ER-ER-ER-ER-ERRR" sounds. Now, I don't know if you have ever had your head in a bucket when a rooster crowed beside you, but it is a very loud experience! I jumped. My poll hit the bucket, and the handle on it bounced and popped up over my head. When I moved to the side, the bucket moved with me! I ran backward, and so did the bucket! I ran forward, but

that was a mistake, because my front leg stuck in the bucket. From there, it all "went downhill," for I couldn't get loose!

I ran around the chicken coop and bumped into chickens, who set to flying and squawking. I ran outside on my three good legs and started spinning. Chickens still were flying everywhere! "Ba-CAWK!" they screamed. It was really loud, because I still had my head in that bucket. Then I screamed, "Maaa-AAA!" and I scared myself! Oats spun everywhere! My heart was pounding! I was exhausted! I just stopped. I gave up. I knew it was over: my first day had been my last.

I collapsed to the ground, the bucket over my head and one front leg still stuck in it. The chickens were racing around and squawking. Rooster C. had spent the entire time watching from the top of a cinder block and saying, "Chuck, chuck, chuck, chuck, chuck," and I recognized this sound as laughter. How could he stand and laugh when I was experiencing my last moments on earth?

Things were quieting down a little. I was thankful that I would be allowed to go in peace. Then I heard the muffled sound of Tacy's voice and, at the same time, another "ER-ER-ER-ER-ERRR!" right next to me! I jumped up and sprang into action, ready for one last fight. Once I was up, I began spinning to see if I could fling the bucket off, but when I did, I walloped old Rooster C. and knocked him to the ground. He jumped up and flapped, and the other chickens began their squawking again. He squawked with them. Feathers flew again, and the oats completely emptied from my bucket.

About that time, my Tacy said, "Ohhh, poor little Izzy!"

I heard the latch on the gate open, and I stopped and stood, shaking. Tacy picked me up and calmly moved the handle over my horn buttons, back toward my nose, and down off my leg. Then she dropped the bucket and rubbed my head.

I was saved! I could see and hear and breathe again! After that, Tacy always snapped my buckets to a hook on the wall or to the fence so that they were no longer a danger to me or to the chickens.

*Courtesies of a small and trivial character are the ones which strike deepest in the grateful and appreciating heart. –* Henry Clay

## 15. I MUST BE A CHICKEN

Identity is important to all kids. I knew I was different, but I didn't know what I was. All I wanted was to belong.

Life on the farm was great. I became used to waking up to the sound of Rooster C. each morning. I would watch as he clucked to the other chickens (Tacy called them "hens"), and they would jump down from their roosts and go with him into the yard of the coop. Rooster C. would cluck to them and then dig and scratch a little while, and then cluck to them again. They would run to where he was and eat whatever he had scratched up. He would stand guard over them and then find a new spot and repeat the scene.

At first, when I would go to see what he was doing, he would drop one wing, dragging the ground with it and walking sideways, like he was sweeping with it. He was really just gathering all the girls and keeping them away from me. I think he may still have been mad about the bucket. I learned just to sleep in for a little while until the sun was higher and warmer.

Surprisingly, one day Rooster C. didn't want me to wait. He came to my corner and crowed. He crowed again, and again, until I got up and stretched. When I did, he got behind me and did his little sweeping motion, herding me out to the other chickens. Next, he pecked around in the chicken feeder and on the ground and herded me over to that. He wanted me to eat, but Tacy hadn't been there with the raisins yet. Rooster C. spilled more of the scratch grain out of the feeder and then clucked to me and to the hens. They came running and pecked up the grain. Rooster C. got behind me and herded me to the grain again. He wouldn't rest until I nibbled a piece. When I did, the whole flock went up in clucks! They were celebrating my first breakfast with them.

About midmorning Tacy would open the gate to

the coop to let the chickens out. I would usually follow her around and trip her while I was trying to help her with her chores, but this morning was different. Rooster C. stayed between Tacy and me. He kept herding me toward his hens, and that day, I went with him.

We spent the morning near the garden, which, by this time, I had learned to avoid because of the strange motions my presence there caused Tacy to make. By midafternoon we had made rounds in the barn, under the shade tree in the yard, and in the garage, where we took a dirt bath and then lay out in the sun for a sunbath.

Throughout the day the hens would go to the coop to lay their eggs, announcing their accomplishment with squawks and clucks. Rooster C. would cluck and crow back to them, and they would rejoin the flock. By evening we were back at the coop. Of course, throughout the day when I saw Tacy, I made sure to say hello and let her rub my face, but Rooster C. always came to retrieve me and gather me into the flock.

That night I lay down in my corner, but that was not where he wanted me. Rooster C. had picked out a cinder block for me. He wouldn't rest until I had put my front hooves on the block. I had my tail toward the wall and my head was aligned with all the other hens when Rooster C. finally took his spot on the roost near me. I thought, "Hmmm, I must be a chicken..." and I drifted off to sleep.

*One is taught by experience to put a premium on those few people who can appreciate you for what you are.*
*– Gail Godwin*

## 16. MULBERRIES

My diet still wasn't what Tacy thought it should be. She was always offering me alfalfa hay, or Sudan hay, or oats, or barley, or "horse and mule" feed. I always wondered why she tried that when it plainly said, "horse and mule," not "goat," on the side of the bag. She still bought raisins for me and still complained about the cost. The wrinklies were always topdressed on my oats or whatever else she might be trying to feed me.

I ate Johnson grass whenever I could find it. I ate leaves off the trees that I could reach, and when I could sneak in, I still liked the red and white flowers in the yard. Rooster C. always offered me bugs – or "insects," to be exact. I heard Tacy explain to James that they weren't "bugs" but "insects," because they had six legs instead of eight. Being an intelligent animal, I quickly adapted to new knowledge. I tasted one once, a choice June beetle, but it really was awful after the crunch, and I snorted and sneezed and spit until the taste was gone.

One day the flock and I were near the yard. Tacy was running what she called the "lawn mower," which really made no sense at all, because she cut the grass and raked it, and then she bagged it and carried it to the horses. I never understood why she didn't just put the horses in the yard. She tried it once but came running at them shortly afterward, yelling something about her flowers. I don't eat grass; not from the ground, at least. I prefer to browse at my eye level or above, not graze. Anyway, Tacy was mowing the grass, and I have to admit that it smelled pleasant. Every now and then, she would pass under the tree in the front yard, and when she did, the sweetest smell would drift my way. It was similar to that of a wrinklie, but fresher. I was drawn to it.

I went to the back gate and pressed my head against it. I had horns about an inch long on the top of my head by now. It seemed a little odd to me, because none of the other chickens had horns or four legs, and I was much taller than they...oh well, they didn't seem to mind. Now, back to that sweet smell...I pressed on the gate, and it gave enough for me to get my head through, which meant that I could wedge the rest of my body through, too. So I did.

I peeped around the corner of the porch just in time to see Tacy rounding the corner into the front yard. I listened as the mower went farther away. Then I sniffed. The aroma of the grass and something sweet mingled together, but the sweetness overpowered the grass and drew me to the large tree in the yard.

I stepped in them first. They were gooey and purple and slippery, and in only a few moments I found myself on the ground in the middle of them, on my side with my legs in the air. Afterwards, a calmness came over me, and I succumbed to relaxation. I lowered my head to the ground and just breathed in the sweetness of the little, purple, bumpy fruits lying there. My nose was right next to one. I sniffed and sniffed. I opened my eyes. I admired the little purple fruit and sniffed some more. And then, it happened: as a reflex, my tongue popped out and licked the little fruit. It was fabulous! I ate it. Then I ate three more that I could reach without moving.

I jumped to my feet and looked around. There were hundreds, maybe thousands, even millions of the little berries! They were on the ground and in the tree. The sunlight glistened through the branches and hit them just right, and then a breeze sent their sweet smell to my nostrils. I jumped for joy – a jump which, of course, put me back on my side amid the juicy berries, my feet in the air. Oh well, at least it was the opposite side.

I heard the mower stop. I got to my feet again and called to Tacy to come and share the treasure I had found. She came around the side of the house and began to laugh. It had taken her so long that I had eaten ten or twelve more and fallen again. She walked over to the porch and sat on the steps. I ran to her, then back to the berries and ate some more. I could eat them off the ground; I could eat them on my side; I could even stand on my hind legs and eat them off the low branches weighted down by their abundance. They were wonderful!

Tacy brought out her box with the flashing light. I wasn't sure what the box did, but I knew she expected a pose. I stretched my back leg out and bowed my neck. I reached around to scratch a spot on my back – and saw that I had purple spots all over my body! I wondered if I were sick! I wondered

if I had contracted a disease from the berries! I wondered if this was my time to go!

I rubbed on the tree trunk and the porch posts and on Tacy, but the spots stayed. I knew I would be purple forever. Tacy just laughed and said, "Oh, Izzy, what would we do without you to entertain us?"

"Entertain! Entertain? My certain death from the

Purple Spot Fever was entertaining?" I thought.

"Come here a minute," said Tacy.

"I will not," I thought, and darted away – to slip in the berries and go down again.

Laughing, Tacy said, "Izzy, you will be completely purple if you keep rolling in those berries!"

I looked around. There were more spots and smudges on my sides and knees and belly. It was the berries, not the Purple Spot Fever! I was going to live!

The best part about the berries was that Tacy did not seem to mind if I ate them. For many days I spent hours in the yard, nibbling berries and napping in between meals. I would stand with my front hooves against the tree and reach into it for berries. I would bend my head backward some-times, and Tacy, finding this entertaining, would come and reward me by pulling a branch down to my reach. The chickens came to enjoy the bountiful harvest. At night when we went to roost, I would smile at their purple beaks and how they matched my purple lips.

*True happiness consists not in the multitude of friends,*
*but in the worth and choice.*
– Ben Jonson

## 17. CHICKEN SNAKE!

One night Rooster C. awoke me with a start. It was not his usual crow. It was a squawk of terror! The chickens crowded quickly to opposite ends of the roost, avoiding the middle.

Now, I don't know if you know it or not, but chickens lay eggs. Rooster C. didn't lay them, but all of his hens did. They each laid one egg every day, and believe it or not, Tacy said they could do that for up to 280 days each year. The hens gladly allowed Tacy to gather their eggs, but lately, she had permitted a few to "set" their nests. This meant that they would hatch chicks after twenty-one days of setting the nests. So, you see, several of the nest boxes had eggs in them.

From my position I could not see what was frightening the chickens. So lowering my feet off my cinder-block roost, I slowly moved toward them. I was almost at the boxes when I saw the thing they feared! I wasn't sure what it was, but I knew it was bad. It was long and black and had beady eyes. When I peeked at its head, I saw that it had its jaws extended over an egg!

This was not good! I screamed at it, "MAAAAA!" but it just lay there, motionless, with the egg in its mouth. The other chickens were in a panic. A few had jumped down and were wandering around the coop, bumping into corners in the dark. There was still a small bulb in the brood lamp, and it made just enough light to allow me to see. Chickens don't usually see in the dark, and knowing that, their predators come at night-and this predator was scary!

I thought for a moment and then knew what I had to do: I had to get out and find Tacy! The gate was latched and would not budge. I couldn't fly out (despite my relationship to the chickens). Then I saw it: a bottom-up five-gallon bucket beneath the low part of the coop fence! I ran to that bucket and jumped onto it, then from it to the top of the fence where I gained my balance on a post before jumping down into the world on the other side.

I ran as fast as I could, hearing the chickens squawking loudly behind me. It wasn't long before I reached the porch and skidded into the front door. I hardly noticed the shadows and night sounds. My flock was in danger and must be saved! I reared up and pounded my front hooves on the door.

Tacy and Mark opened it almost immediately. They looked surprised to see me. Timbra poked her nose out, heard the chickens, and sounded the alarm! Tacy grabbed some shoes and headed out the door with me as Mark yelled, "I'll get the gun!" I ran back through the open yard gate and toward the chicken house with Timbra just in front of me and Tacy just behind. When we reached the chicken coop, Tacy flung the gate open. It took only seconds for her to see the egg thief and spring into action! She and Timbra made quite a team. The scene that followed is not for the weak.

Tacy panicked when she saw the snake, yelling, "SNAKE!" Timbra was barking at it but couldn't get to it. Tacy grabbed the snake by its tail and flung it to the ground. Then Timbra grabbed it and shook it. Egg juice went everywhere! The snake moved no more.

We all felt bad about the death of the snake. Timbra took it in her teeth and carried it outside the coop and off into the tall weeds. I realized that life on the farm is tough, especially for what they call "varmints" and "snakes." I looked out the door of the coop and saw Mark. He was wearing his boots and a pair of shorts, and he had his hat and gun. I knew I was safe. No one said anything else; everyone knew things would be okay. Tacy and Mark locked the gates back and headed toward the house as I found my cinder-block roost.

*True friendship comes when silence between two people is comfortable.* – David Tyson Gentry

## 18. MONSTER CHARLIE IS BACK!

It had been a long time since I had thought about the monster, Charlie. In fact, I had forgotten about him. But today, he would be etched in my mind forever.

It was a normal day. I had made most of the rounds with the flock and was a blissful five or ten minutes into my afternoon nap, dreaming in the warm sunshine and soaking in its rays. It was wonderful...until my dream changed. I thought I could feel something very close to me, and I could hear loud breathing. As I roused to consciousness, I could feel hot, powerful breaths on my back blowing the hair forward!

My eyes popped open. I did not move. My eyes looked forward and could see nothing. They looked to the side, and then to the other side, and still saw nothing. I turned my head ever so slightly to the rear, and that's when I saw it: Monster Charlie, looking right at me!

He continued to inhale and exhale and push

gently against my back. I knew that if I ran, he could catch me, so I chose to be perfectly still. Then, as though his warm, damp breaths were not enough, he stuck out a long, rough tongue and licked my back against the grain. That was it! I was out of there, crying, "Maaaa!" all the way to Tacy.

I thought I had escaped Monster Charlie, but he was in hot pursuit – well, kind of "cool" pursuit, actually, as he was just walking to catch up with me.

"What is it, Izzy?" asked Tacy. I stood by her and trembled as he came closer. "What? Is it Charlie?"

Death approached us both, and she stood idly wondering what it was!

"Izzy, Charlie won't hurt you. Mark let him into the pasture again until fall. You will have to get used to him."

"Used to him!" I thought. I ran behind Tacy's legs. Charlie was upon us now, and Tacy reached out to him. He sniffed her hand. Looking up from between her knees at Charlie looking down at me, I saw a big wet nose followed by a gray face, big black eyes, and a great big hump. He had four legs with heavy black cloven hooves at the ends of them. He was gray all over, not just on his face.

He swung his head around and threw slobber on his hump. Flies moved away from his face and legs to the dampened hump. When he looked back at me, he stuck out his tongue and licked a nostril in his broad, wet nose. Then he licked the other one. Then he licked my head!

Yuck! He licked me after he licked his nose! It was gross to think about, but wait! – it really felt soothing. He did it again and again, until Tacy ordered, "Okay, Charlie, that's enough." Then, "How about some rubbing for my favorite Brahman bull?" She stepped away from me and toward Charlie and began to rub his head, neck, and shoulders. She rubbed his back and around his tail. Next, she rubbed his belly, and his head slowly dropped. His knees buckled, and down he dropped to the ground! As she kept rubbing his belly, he rolled to his side and stuck his legs straight out. I thought she had killed him until he made a strange sound, almost like snoring.

"Come on over, Izzy, and give him a sniff. He'll sleep until I quit rubbing." I did walk over, and I sniffed and pawed at him a little, but he just slumbered on. He was a giant! I was about the size of his head, and Tacy was only as tall as his shoulders. It would have taken fifteen of her to equal his size... yet there he lay, asleep, snoring, and content.

Monster? I don't think so.

*Yes'm, old friends is always best, 'less you can catch a new one that's fit to make an old one out of.*
*– Sarah Orne Jewett*

## 19. ONLY HOME AT NIGHT

After that, it wasn't long before James left in a car with his parents. Tacy and Mark loaded up horses in trailers and sent them to other people. Tacy spent more time near the house and rested in the evenings. I would sit with her on the porch while my flock finished their rounds. It was one of my favorite times. Timbra enjoyed it with us. She stretched out flat on the cool concrete of the porch, and when I spoke softly with a "maaa," she responded with a wag of her tail. Tacy would take turns rubbing each of us.

Sometimes Mark would join in, and even a cat or two would come up from the barn. Charlie would low in the pasture, but no cows would answer, only coyotes in the distance.

The berries were long gone from the tree, and my appetite had increased so much that I had developed a taste for oats. On occasion, I even stuck my head in the "horse and mule" bag for a nibble. My horns were about two inches long now and were beginning to curve ever so slightly. I was much taller than the rest of my flock. I was almost as big as Timbra, in fact.

One morning Tacy left in her car and didn't come home all day. That evening, when she did come home, she brought a lot of books with her. She talked about "Agricultural Economics" and "Teaching Strategies for the Agricultural Classroom." She spent a lot of time reading in the evenings and on weekends, and every weekday, she loaded up her car and was gone all day.

Tacy's daily absence meant more responsibility for Timbra and me. Someone had to make sure the chickens were safe. Someone had to walk the perimeters of the barn and outbuildings to make certain they were not invaded. Someone had to make sure the horses stayed out of the yard. Basically, someone had to take charge. I was that someone.

Timbra helped out when she could. She would come whenever I called and bravely battle fierce stinging scorpions, skunks, and 'possums. Sometimes, she would take off after a rabbit and leave me to tend the farm alone.

We always checked the feed-room door on our perimeter walks, and if it was open, we tested the feed for freshness. Sometimes Mark would get home and find us in there, and if he did, he never seemed too happy. Sometimes Mark would sit on the porch with us and wait for Tacy. The three of us would watch down the driveway until her car appeared. She seemed to get a kick out of our watching for her from the porch.

"How was school today?" Mark would ask.

"Good. I learned so much. I hope I can remember it all," Tacy might answer.

"You will. It's just a few months until you graduate next May."

"Then what?" Tacy often wondered aloud.

My answer would be a "maaaa," hoping that then things would return to normal. They didn't...but things were still good. We sat on the porch until dark, when Tacy walked me to the coop.

*The happiest moments of my life have been the few which I have passed at home in the bosom of my family.*
*– Thomas Jefferson*

## 20. A CHANGE IN THE SEASONS

The days grew shorter in the fall, and strange things began to happen. Charlie was the first to notice the days' length, and he jumped the fence into the next field where Mark's cows grazed the wheat he had planted. He let Charlie stay, as it would only have been about two more weeks before he moved him anyway. The horses started growing thicker hair, and so did I – but the rest of my flock looked terrible!

You see, chickens molt. They lose their feathers every fall. Now, don't worry, they get them back, and then they look all fresh and new. But for a while, they are naked. They have only a few straggling feathers here and there.

I didn't know why my hair should be different. I made the same rounds as they did. Rooster C. took the same good care of me as he did the others, and I roosted with them, now earlier each night. Yet, I never molted.

The days got shorter and the temperature cooler, but with my new thicker coat, I hardly noticed. Mark would feed earlier now, before Tacy got home. Mark and I had a different relationship than my Tacy and I did. Like Tacy, he seemed to enjoy my company, but he would grab my horns and shake them, and I would get angry and butt him with my head. Then he would shake me by the horns, and I would butt him again. It became a game to see who could catch the other off guard. Timbra played, too, allowing us to chase her tail as she joined in the fun. This was "roughhousing" at its best. I know, because that's what Mark called it when Tacy drove up each night, and we had to quit.

The grass turned brown, and the garden died. Tacy let me eat the brown flowers in the yard that had faded from the bright colors of spring and summer. Birds flew overhead in the shape of a "V" that was pointed south. The leaves left their home on the trees and fell to the ground. I discovered a new favorite for my menu: dried leaves.

When it got even colder, Tacy and Mark put up lights and carried a cotton stalk inside. They decorated it with little balls and elves and lights and ribbon. I could see the lights on the house at night through a crack in the wall of the chicken coop.

One morning, I woke to find myself dusted in white cold. I stood and shook, and it fell to the ground. Outside the door the ground was completely covered with the stuff. It was very beautiful; I had never seen anything so clean. Tacy didn't leave that day, and all of us played in the white stuff all day long. At first I was afraid, but Tacy coaxed me out into it, and it was just plain fun to jump up and down in leaps and bounds, then drop into the fluffy cold.

She rolled up balls of the stuff and threw them at me, and then I chased her. She rolled up one big ball, and another, and before long there was a round stranger, three balls high, in the yard. I kept my distance. Tacy added a hat, some rocks for eyes and a mouth, and sticks for arms. I knew then that it wasn't real, so I approached. I grabbed a stick arm with my teeth and pulled...off it came!

I ran away, then came back to grab the other one, and it came off, too. Then I put my front feet on the stranger's chest and reached for the hat on his head. I stretched, but I wasn't tall enough. I backed up to take another look at the situation. I made a running start, and when I got to the big stranger, I jumped, and all my four feet landed in his midsection where I pushed off and reached for the hat on my way up. I missed and wound up rolling in the white cold. Recovering, I took a longer run and jumped sooner and straighter up to boost off his midsection harder, but I missed the hat on the way up. That was okay, though, because I knocked it off with my feet on the way back down...along with his head. This was fun! I backed up, ran forward, and jumped on top of what remained of the man. There I stood, queen of the white, cold world!

That's when Tacy came back out with her flashing black box. I struck a proud pose. She did make the box flash, but while I was posing for a second flash, I was hit by what Tacy called a "snowball." It knocked me from my coveted spot. I remounted, bowed my neck, and put my head down against the next attack, which shortly came. Tacy put her capped head against mine and started to push! I pushed back and she pushed back, then with a laugh she moved very quickly aside, just as I pushed with extra strength...needless to say, losing my footing and finishing with legs to the sky in the white cold! Tacy helped me up, saying, "Let's get that snow off you, Izzy."

So that's what they call white cold: "snow." Well, it wasn't much fun when I was upside down in it! The wind blew my belly hair and drafted sharply in.

"Come on, girl," said Tacy. "Let's haul some water." I hadn't thought about being thirsty, but found I was. We headed to the house where I was invited into the kitchen. I knew not to go beyond the slick floor of the kitchen, but I stuck my head around the corner and checked out the people-house. Tacy had five-gallon buckets and was filling them with water from the kitchen sink. When they were full, she started out the door. "Come on, Izzy," she instructed.

Outside, misty steam rose from the buckets Tacy carried. We started with the chicken coop and then the horse lot. Back we had to go, then, for more water from the house. Tacy said she wished the pipes were thawed. The next buckets went across the fence to Charlie, and we carried more to the horses. Finally, we gave some to the cats. Timbra drank her water in the house. This water-toting was tough work, and I was exhausted that night when I crawled onto my roost. The other chickens had stayed in that day and were already roosting. Rooster C. clucked a welcome to me. I tried to lie down, but he clucked and squawked until I took my spot on the cinder-block roost, where my head bobbed, and I drifted into my dreams.

*Winter, a lingering season, is a time to gather golden moments, embark upon a sentimental journey and enjoy every idle hour.* – John Boswell

## 21. SPRING!

Winter seemed a long time in passing that year, but spring finally came. It rained a lot. I spent days inside the coop with the chickens while Tacy was away at her school and while Mark worked. Timbra made her rounds faithfully and wagged her tail at me as we sniffed noses through the fence. Rain didn't seem to bother her, but it was tough on us chickens.

Flowers began to pop their heads up, and birds returned to our land. Green grass began to grow. I remembered the flowers and the berries from last summer. I checked the yard for them on pretty days, but they were not there yet. Tacy planted in her garden, but it was fenced now, so I couldn't help much.

It was early May when Tacy graduated from her school. There was a big celebration and strangers came to the house and said things like "Congratulations!" and "What a cute goat!" I didn't even know we had a goat; in fact, I knew there was no goat! City folks! What to do with them...they couldn't even get their goats and chickens straight!

Days returned to almost normal. They got warmer and longer, and Tacy was home almost every day. Life was good. Broody hens hatched baby peeps. There was a new foal in the horse lot. The barn cat had kittens. Timbra and I were in charge of them all, and we made quite a team. I stayed with the hens and chicks and butted away the cats who made attempts to snatch a chick for a tasty morsel. Timbra made rounds early in the morning to make sure the coyotes kept their distance from the horse pens and the chickens. Rooster C. kept a watchful eye and responded with a "Ba-caw!" each time a chick peeped in distress.

The garden grew. The grass grew...and grew... and grew! The leaves thickened on the trees, and the mulberry tree in the front yard bloomed, promising a good season for the purple treats. Spring had sprung!

*What joy or sadness often springs from just the simple little things!* – Willa Hoey

## 22. COPPERHEAD!

Some of the most dangerous things in life strike with no warning. One day, about eleven in the morning, that time just before the sun is straight above us in the sky, Timbra and the barn dogs sounded the alarm by a bush. Since they needed my help, I left my post by the chickens and peeps to head in their direction. When I got to them, the three dogs – Timbra, her friend Dobie, and a barn dog named Binky – had the bush surrounded. They were standing back from it about four feet and barking really loudly.

I couldn't see a thing by the bush. There was some tall grass, but that was all. I heard the door of the house open and close, and Tacy stepped out to see what was going on. The dogs kept barking, and I heard Tacy holler, "Snake bark!" as she ran back into the house.

"Snake bark?" I puzzled. I went up behind Timbra and nudged her – and she almost jumped out of her skin! In a chain reaction, the other dogs jumped, then yelped and shied away. They turned and came right back as soon as they realized it was only Izzy, the simple chicken.

I decided I would have to be the brave one,

because when they did come back, they still kept their distance from the bush. It was a small mesquite with only a few leaves on it. The brown grass with new green shoots was thick around its base, and a prickly pear cactus grew beside it. I could not see a snake, and I knew snakes! After all, I had faced the egg-stealer in the chicken coop. Timbra had defeated it single-handedly. Why did she think this snake, wherever it was, would be any different?

By this time, Tacy was hurrying down the steps with her .22 pistol, hopping as she pulled on her boots. I would have to speak to her about some rules of safety, but that could wait, because I had a snake to find and defeat!

I marched to the bush, and as I did, I felt something grab my leg! I turned to find Timbra, gently trying to pull me back. I told her to let go, but again she pulled back on me. (She was very gentle with her teeth, and though they were pinching me, they never broke the skin.) How exasperating! Again, I asked her to let go, and when she didn't, I pulled forward. She lost her grip, and I made a hard landing right into that bush, almost belly up. I was still on the ground, trying to steady myself, when I noticed it was quiet. The dogs, heads cocked to one side, were staring at me. I glanced around and saw

Tacy running toward me with that gun...I really would have to talk to her about safety.

The dogs whined, pulling my attention back to the mess I had not yet realized I was in. Timbra moved around by the cactus and reached out with her paw to dig a little beside my leg. Then she sat down, cocked her head, and fixed her eyes on the spot where she had been digging. I followed her stare down to my right. In the fold of my leg was the head of a snake! Its nose was pointed away from my body. It was a snub-nosed head, and the rust-colored skin of it had light tan markings. It was wedged tightly in the angle made by my folded knee. It was then that I felt the snake's body beneath mine and looked to the left. I could not know how much of the snake was under me, but about three feet of its body was sticking out from under my left side – and it was beginning to wriggle! The other dogs sat down, whined, and cocked their heads from side to side.

"Hmmmm. What to do? Don't panic...DON'T PANIC?! Are you nuts?" I said to myself. Here I lay, with a poisonous snake beneath me (only later did I learn about the poison), and I could feel it wrapped around my leg! I looked down at the copper patterns on its back, and my eyes followed the

patterns all the way to the tip of its green tail. I thought back to when the dogs had been barking, and I had first looked at the bush...I had seen this tail! But I had thought it was a part of the tree and the clump of grass. What a predicament!

Tacy finally came. It had taken her at least thirty or forty seconds...she would have to work on her emergency response time! She looked over the situation. Confused, the dogs wagged their tails and whined. Tacy looked from one side of my body to the other, then she backed away and squatted down to think. It was during her thinking time that I felt the thorns from the mesquite bush prodding me in my side and started to shift my position.

"Izzy, don't move!" commanded Tacy. I obeyed. Tacy rose and called Timbra over. "Timbra, do you want to get a snake?" she asked, while scratching Timbra's head. Timbra responded with a big wag of her tail.

Hoping she and Timbra had a plan, I stayed very still while Tacy put her booted heel hard on the head of the snake that was stuck in the crook of my leg. Then she reached down, stood my back end up, and removed the coiled snake from my legs. Timbra watched and waited.

Tacy lifted me up into her arms and ordered, "Sic 'em, Timbra!" As Tacy jumped away from the snake's head, Timbra grabbed close to its tail and gave that snake a good snap and a shake and a snap! It lay still on the ground. That's when the other dogs moved in and imitated Timbra, taking the snake into the weeds to dispose of it.

Timbra trotted over to Tacy and me and sniffed and wagged. Tacy praised her and patted her, and then she patted me. "Come on, you two. Let's get a treat. Izzy, I have some raisins for you, and a Milkbone for you, Timbra."

I understood what had just happened and how

close to death I had come. I stayed right beside Timbra as we started for the house.

*A faithful friend is a strong defense;*
*and he that hath found such a one*
*hath found a treasure.*
– Alfred, Lord Tennyson

## 23. MOVING!

Summer was back! The berries were almost ripe! It was warm. Well, really it was hot, but I didn't care, because my coat was slick and shiny, and all the heavy winter hair was gone. I had rubbed it off in the spring on the fence in the chicken coop.

Tacy came home one day and seemed excited. She didn't say much to me or to Timbra. We knew she was waiting for Mark to get there. When he finally came, she ran to him and told him that she had a "job". She was excited, so we were, too. She told him it was in Woodson and that she started in August. He responded that it was great and that he would call his uncle and see if they could rent the old farmhouse his granddad used to own. Then he asked, "What about all the animals?"

"What about them?" was Tacy's response.

"Well," answered Mark, "what will we do with them?"

"Do with them? Well, they're moving, too!" and she more or less skipped up the steps and into the house.

"Moving?" I thought. What was "moving"? Mark stood there with his cap in his hand, looking at us and scratching his head. He must have wondered what "moving" was, too. I tried to tell all the animals that we were "moving," but they all continued in their daily routines. For days I told them we were going somewhere, because that's what "moving" is: going somewhere else. However, they seemed to chuckle at me. I stayed close to Tacy, because I didn't want to be left behind. Everywhere she went, I went. I stayed right beside her, and I mean right beside her. Timbra was there, too, wondering what we were doing.

Tacy packed boxes and moved furniture into one room and then packed more boxes. A couple of times she locked me up in the chicken coop and left with a car full of boxes. The first time I thought she had moved without me! But she came home with the boxes gone from her car.

She packed more, and I stood in the yard and fretted and ate berries that were just beginning to ripen. She made another trip. Then, one weekend, she and Mark were gone together. They took two vehicles packed full of boxes, and a neighbor came to feed us; well, those of us who remained. (Timbra and Dobie had gone with Tacy and Mark.)

On that Monday, Mark came back, but Tacy was gone! She had moved without me! She had moved without Mark! I couldn't believe it. I moped everywhere. Mark tried to cheer me, but it was no use. I lost my appetite. Berries weren't even tasty, and raisins were not the same from Mark. I lay in the corner of the coop and didn't care if Rooster C. expected me to be on my roost. Tacy was gone.

By Friday, things seemed grim...until I heard it: Tacy's car, coming down the driveway! I bounced up and ran onto the porch from which I could see over the yard fence and further down the driveway. There!...Timbra's head was sticking out the window! And I could see Tacy in the driver's seat. I jumped for joy, straight up...and straight down onto the slippery porch, where I found myself flattened and flailing to recover my footing. Mark had heard Tacy's approach and made it to the porch just in time to witness my landing-gear failure. He laughed and then started waving to Tacy as she pulled into the carport.

Timbra flew through the window and ran to Mark and then to me, licking and panting. Dobie was glad to see all of us, too. Then, there she was! My Tacy was kneeling down, holding raisins! I ran as fast as I could, and this time, she was flat, on the ground with me atop her, eating raisins while she laughed.

Her first week of teaching had gone well. On Sunday night she loaded more things into her dad's borrowed El Camino and hooked up the trailer. She loaded a horse and some feed and put the dogs in the car. I stood and watched, waiting to be left behind again. But Mark rounded the corner with a pen of chickens and Rooster C. and said, "Come on, Izzy. You're going to Woodson!"

I was moving!

*Life can only be understood backwards, but it must be lived forwards.* – Soren Kierkegaard

## 24. I AM STILL A CHICKEN!

It was a long ride. I could see only parts of the trip through the slats in the trailer. It was hot and dusty. The chickens panted. When at last the truck slowed down, the horse pricked its ears forward and looked from side to side. I could see a farmhouse down a long drive and a dirt water tank and a small barn to the left of the house. All the grass was dry and dead here. Everything was dusty. The truck halted in front of a house.

Timbra and Dobie ran around and jumped up on the back of the trailer. Timbra's friendly tongue let me know everything was okay. Tacy joined us and opened the back gate of the trailer. "Come on, Izzy, it's your new home," she said, with her reassuring smile. I looked out the back of the trailer. It was really brown around this place, and the leaves were thin on the trees. Tacy patted me and eased me out of the trailer. The ground felt dry, and the land had cracks in it. It was hot.

Tacy brought a wheelbarrow, loaded the cage of chickens into it, and wheeled it down to a place under the shade on one side of the barn. I tagged along. There was a pen behind the barn with wire from floor to ceiling, and inside the pen was a door that opened into the barn. Tacy headed back to the trailer to unload the horse, and I went to help her. We brought the horse back down to the barn and led it through the lot and into the pasture where we turned it loose and watched it run. How beautiful! It was a stocky little bay horse, almost black, with a black mane and tail that blew as it ran. Dust flew behind it as it trailed along the fence, checking out its new surroundings.

Timbra and Dobie appeared from over a hill near the barn, a hill that made the edge of the dirt tank. They had muddy paws and were panting. Tacy headed up the hill of the tank dam. I went, too. She almost tripped over me several times, because she was staying so close to me...she must have been worried about the new surroundings, too. At the top of the hill, Tacy stopped. There wasn't much water in the tank, and the water that was there was brown. Tacy shook her head and said, "Izzy, if you pray, ask for an end to this drought." So, from then on, I prayed for the end of the drought.

It was a hot, muggy August evening, and the sun was beginning to set behind the barn. I watched the barn become a silhouette along with the horse in the distance behind it. I was tired. Tacy must have sensed that, because she patted me and said, "Come on, girl. Let's get you and your flock settled." She grabbed a plastic bucket and went to the water's edge to fill it as best she could, with as little mud as possible. I didn't go too close, as I might have gotten my feet dirty, and I can't stand dirty feet! We carried the water bucket back to the barn. By crowing, Rooster C. expressed his disdain of the fact that he was still in the cage.

"Just a minute, Rooster C.," said Tacy. "I'm getting your new home ready." She continued to be busy, filling water pans within the wire pen. Then she came out of the pen, opened a door that seemed to be part of the wall, and stepped through it into the barn. She pulled the string to open a sack of hen scratch and scooped two cans of it into a feed bucket. Back to the pen with that bucket she went, to pour some scratch into several feeders there. The other chickens observed thoughtfully. Rooster C. exclaimed, "Ba-caw!" to let Tacy know he was ready to be free. There was a door on the wire pen, and Tacy made certain it worked before beginning to unload Rooster C. and his flock.

I was so tired. I longed for the safety and familiarity of my little cinder block and the cool, shady coop back home. I wanted to eat berries from the mulberry tree and flowers from the yard, even if Tacy yelled at me. Here, there were no flowers and no mulberries; there wasn't even very much water. I suppose I had taken for granted the water from the well at home. Timbra was too busy making safety inspections here to play with me. I was so very tired....

"Izzy, your turn."

"Maaa," I answered, asking, "What turn?"

"I know you're homesick, but your new place is here." The chickens milled around within the wire pen, pecking at scratch grains and listening to Rooster C. He herded them to different corners and scratched for them as if nothing had changed. Tacy walked to the door inside the pen that led into the barn. "Come here, Izzy. You'll like this."

I walked to the door. Inside, there were wall boxes and metal roosts. There was a brood lamp in the corner, turned off, of course, for no one needs a brood lamp when it's 108 degrees outside. But the thing that was best, the thing that I wanted the most, Tacy had provided. It was a big hop up, but next to the wall boxes, adjusted to just the right distance from the wall, was a brand new cinder block upon which I was to roost! I went in and took my place, contented. It was a new place, but I was still a chicken, and I was home again.

*A house is built of logs and stone,*
*Of tiles and posts and piers,*
*A home is built of loving deeds*
*That stand a thousand years.*
– Victor Hugo

## 25. COYOTES

Chickens will roost in the same place every night once they are taught where to roost. Tacy kept us locked up in the wire pen for three days before we were allowed out. Even then, for two days more, she let us out only in the evenings until she was certain we would make it back to the wire pen. Each day she let us out when she got home from school, and each evening she locked us in. Timbra and Dobie were there to protect us. I helped Tacy clean up around the place.

One evening, as she and I were working, I felt something watching us. Tacy must have felt it, too, because she looked up at the same time I did. Down by the barn, like a shadow right behind the chicken coop, was a coyote. Rooster C. had seen him and had begun gathering the girls. Tacy and I ran toward the intruder, screaming and "maaaaa-ing," and the coyote tucked his tail and ran. Rooster C. had just put the last of the girls inside, and I gladly joined them – quickly! quickly! – as Tacy shut and locked the gate.

Timbra and Dobie had been napping and woke, wondering what the commotion was. Tacy pointed Timbra's head in the direction of the vanishing coyote and said, "Sic 'em, Timbra." She cued right in on him and streaked away to catch him! Dobie was in hot pursuit. When the coyote saw them coming, he doubled his speed, cleared under the fence, and was out of sight. Timbra stuck her nose in the air and barked, then started back to Tacy.

That night, it sounded like a jamboree in the surrounding pastures. Coyotes yipped and hollered, yapped and howled, and Timbra and Dobie answered back with long, low moans and growls. It was very unsettling. After that, Tacy turned us out of our pen later in the day and then kept us closer to the barn and farther from the coyotes.

*A day of worry is more exhausting than a week of work.*
— John Lubbock

## 26. RUCKUS

Life was pretty simple as a chicken...at least until I found out that I was a goat!

One weekend, Mark's uncle Jamie from Breckenridge, brought a huge animal to stay with us. He was brown and had a black stripe down his back. He had a big Roman nose, long, pendulous ears, and a little short tail. He had four legs and cloven hooves. He wasn't "big" like kind, old Monster Charlie was big, but he was big for a chicken: he weighed about three hundred pounds! I was the biggest chicken in the coop until then, and I weighed only 120 pounds. (The rest of the girls knew I was a little self-conscious about my weight since it was fifteen times what each of them weighed, but they never said a squawk about it.)

Meanwhile, when the new animal showed up, Jamie led it down to our wire pen. It snorted and pawed the ground and said, "Muh-la-la-la-la-la-lah." That was the strangest speech I had ever heard. I retreated to the back of our pen and gawked at him. He was offensive. He smelled bad, like musk. Tacy came to the pen and led me out, using the red collar I had been allowed to wear since the move. My horns had grown long and were smooth and curved. When the stranger reached out to smell me and made his awful sound, I bowed my neck, turned my head, and threatened him with my horns. Then I walked away over the tank dam for a drink.

I walked to the edge of the water, where Tacy had made a trail of rocks for me, as I still did not like muddy feet. I was standing there taking a cool drink when I saw a reflection mirrored in the water, a reflection I had never noted before. It was similar to the animal I had seen in the porch window at our other home. It was bigger, with long, slender, smooth horns that curved gently toward its back. It was tan, with a white stripe down its face and black accents around its eyes, nose, knees, and down its back. Its ears didn't quite lie down and didn't quite stand up. Could it be? Was it...?

I was rudely interrupted then as the creature that Jamie had brought ran over the tank dam and down to the water's edge, stopping beside me to have a drink. I glanced in front of him on the water. The reflection in front of him mirrored him exactly. I looked in front of myself and blinked, and my reflection blinked back at me. I moved my head, and so did my reflection.

I didn't know whether to be happy or sad. I didn't know what to think. I realized in that moment that I didn't look like the other chickens. Neither did this big, strange creature. I studied him; I studied my reflection. His eyes were like mine.

Varooom, barooom, vaaarooom! A truck started in the driveway. I ran to the top of the tank dam toward the noise. Jamie was pulling away, and Tacy was waving good-bye to him.

"MAAAAAA!" I screamed, trying to tell him that he had forgotten his beast. "Maaaaaa!" I said to Tacy, telling her to stop him and make him take the creature away. But no one was listening to me except the creature, who was following me everywhere, making his "muh-la-la" sounds and pawing at me. I turned toward him and presented my horns. He countered with the poll of his head, which was as hard as my horns. I ran to the barn, and so did he. I ran to Tacy – and so did he! Jamie's last words as he drove away were, "Take care of my goat!"

"Man," said Tacy, "he's raising quite a ruckus!"

About that time he made a sweep a little too close to her and knocked her flat on the ground. "That's his name, then: Ruckus."

I fled to the barn again, nudged the latch, and ran into the chicken coop. Ruckus missed the gate in, so I had a moment to rest. It gave me time to think about Jamie's words. Ruckus was a goat! Then I must be a goat, too! All this time I had thought I was a chicken, but the evidence of the tank mirror and Jamie's words informed me: I was a goat!

Ruckus started hitting the wire with his head,

wanting in. The chickens screamed, "Ba-caw!" Ruckus continued hitting the wire. Rooster C. was gathering his girls and putting them in a corner. Tacy was dusting off and starting toward the barn.

By the time she got there, Ruckus had made a hole in the wire and was angrily putting his head through, sticking out his tongue at me and making his "muh-la-la" sounds ever more loudly. Tacy tried to pull him back, but he forced his head farther through, and when she swatted him to get his attention, he withdrew his head, stood on his hind legs with neck bowed and eyes rolled...and charged her! Lucky she was fast! He did it again, and this time she ran, and he chased her for a while. (I would never tell Tacy that I laughed at how funny they looked, but I did laugh, just a little.)

Finally, Tacy grabbed a shovel, and when Ruckus reared up, she didn't run. She met his poll with the handle of the shovel, and they both stopped. I had tried to tell her not to let Jamie leave without Old Ruckus, but she had not listened. Once she had stopped him for a moment, she grabbed his beard, dragged him to the barn, and put a collar and a rope on him. She pulled him to a tree on the tank dam, tied him there, and walked away. She was out of breath. It seemed to me that he chuckled a little bit while saying "muh-la-la" and sticking out his tongue.

Tacy said not a word. She just fixed the wire and fed us. She put out water for Ruckus. Then she went to the house. I think her day was over. Timbra and Dobie trailed along behind.

*If you are all wrapped up in yourself,*
*you are overdressed.* – Kate Halverson

## 27. RUCKUS SAVES THE DAY

I thought about my life with the chickens and how good they had been to me. I had spent days with them and roosted with them. Rooster C. had made me a part of his flock, and I was grateful for that. Now this horrible Ruckus had come to our farm, and with him came the realization that I am a goat.

I was still a little afraid of Ruckus, even though he had spent his first week tied to the tree. I would try to get close to him to investigate, but he would stick his tongue out and make a noise and paw, and I would run. Seeing that I did not favor him, Ruckus finally gave up on making friends with me, and after Tacy let him go, he would settle to bed just outside the wire pen. Ruckus was a large Nubian male goat, a "buck". He certainly didn't understand why I preferred the company of chickens to his "sweet" disposition.

When Tacy turned me out in the mornings, I would run as far from Ruckus as I could. He would try to follow, but I could outrun him. He gave up on me fairly quickly, but began chasing people! When Mark came outside, Ruckus would follow him, and when Mark wasn't looking, Ruckus would knock him to the ground. He thought that was great fun! He was very cautious around Tacy, however, for she fed him his meals. Also, he remembered the lesson of the shovel.

Ruckus finally adapted to his lot of being alone at the farm. He went behind the barn to graze while I went with the chickens and did my grazing in front of the barn. Gradually, day by day, Rooster C. would lead us farther and farther behind the barn. Sometimes, I would look up and realize we were actually following Ruckus. As dry as it was, grass was disappearing from the pasture, and Ruckus began reaching through the fence for more to eat. The grass truly was "greener on the other side of the fence." The rest of us followed suit and would put our heads through for the grass on the other side. At night I would guard the door to the barn, but I did let Ruckus come inside the wire pen to bed down.

One morning it was foggy when we woke up. I went with Ruckus and Rooster C. to the fence where the tall grass was. I put my head through the fence – and my collar snagged on the bottom wire! Feeling myself caught, I raised my head and pulled back, but my horns had become so long that they hung on the top wire. I panicked and squirmed and pulled, but I was stuck! My foot then slipped through the wire, putting weight on it. I was choking! I lost my footing and then regained it, but it felt like the wire was getting tighter and tighter. I could only scream "Blaaaaaaa!" because I could not open my mouth!

Ruckus looked up and saw what was happening to me. Knowing only he could bring help, he ran his fastest to the yard, calling for Tacy all the way. Tacy bolted out of the door and onto the porch, hopping around, jerking her clothes on. She knew there was trouble and thought maybe it was a coyote. She ran out into the yard where Ruckus met her at the gate. He stopped her by pushing his head against her, then turned and ran in the direction of the barn. Tacy started back to the house, thinking Ruckus had just been caught eating in the yard – nothing more.

Ruckus knew I was in trouble and that time was short, so he turned back, ran past Tacy into the yard, turned, and stood on his hind feet, bringing his head down to meet her. Then off he went again toward the barn.

Puzzled, Tacy started to follow him. Ruckus returned to her and then back to the barn several times as she walked through the fog. "Izzy?" she called, but I didn't answer. I couldn't answer; I was too weak.

Finally, it struck Tacy that Ruckus was trying to lead her to me! She ran around the corner to the back of the barn just as Ruckus turned the corner on another trip back to her. The collision knocked the wind out of them both. Each stood up; Tacy brushed off and Ruckus shook. Then he took off into the fog toward me. Tacy called to him, and he answered. She followed his voice through the fog and finally saw him standing over something on the ground next to the fence. It was me!

"Izzy!" Tacy ran to me as quickly as she could. I could hardly breathe. Tacy willed herself to stay calm and managed to bend the fence wire and get it off my head. She rubbed my throat and tried to help me stand. She took my collar off. Ruckus looked on and bleated softly to me while Tacy rubbed my throat. Finally, I coughed and, with help, stood up and panted for a moment. Ruckus walked up beside me as I turned. Tacy watched as I leaned on Ruckus and he gently led me to the barn. I knew that Ruckus had saved my life. Suddenly, it seemed as though he was not so bad.

We went back to the coop. Just inside the door, I lay down. Ruckus went around to my back and lay down against me, to support me. I stretched my sore neck out and listened. My head was about even with his shoulder, and I could hear his heartbeat. I remembered the heartbeats in my life: my mother, my Tacy, my Timbra, even the really fast beat of Rooster C.... and now, my Ruckus.

*My only sketch, profile, of Heaven is a large blue sky,*
*a larger sky than the biggest I have seen in June –*
*and in it are my friends – every one of them.*
*– Emily Dickinson*

## 28. TWINS IN THE SPRING

Fall passed that year into a harsh winter. In January we had seventeen days of below-freezing temperatures. Tacy broke the ice on our water for us every day and made sure thatwe were warm and dry. The cold tried to steal into our little barn, but it never could. For a while, Ruckus roosted with me on a cinder block, but then he convinced me that it was more comfortable in the straw pile that Tacy had made for us in the corner. The brooder lamp was on twenty-four hours a day. Ruckus and I huddled under it between feeding time and drinks of water. The chickens would sit on top of us to warm their toes.

Spring couldn't arrive fast enough as far as I was concerned. I wanted warm weather and sunshine. I was feeling rather fat and moving very slowly. The thaw came at the end of February, and March brought days of sixty degrees and nights above freezing. Green grass spiked through the layers of dead grass with the help of the melting ice. The broody hens were getting ready to set their eggs. The days were growing longer.

One day, I felt different. I was anxious. I pawed at the hay in the corner of our pen, but because the sun was shining, I went outside to paw at the ground under a tree still winter-bare and leafless. In no time my pawing had built a hill. I was not sure why I had built the hill, but something inside told me I needed to. I lay down with my chest on top of the hill and my rear end down the hill, and then it happened! I felt a twinge, and my water broke! Suddenly, I knew: I was having a baby!

I called to Tacy, "MAAAAA!" I called to Ruckus, "MAAAAA!" And I called to Timbra, "MAAAAA!" They all came running. They came to the hill where I was lying, and Tacy sprang into action. She ran to the house to grab towels and was back in a flash. She sat patiently while I went through my labor. Timbra lay down with her paws on either side of her face, watching intently. Dobie followed suit. Ruckus stood off from the crowd, but he never stopped watching. He didn't eat or move. He just watched.

At last Tacy said, "Here comes a nose!" She moved in closer and broke the sack around the nose, saying the nose was dark brown like Ruckus's. In about a minute, there came hooves and a head, and in another minute, on the ground was a brown-and-black baby with white on her face! Tacy wiped her off a little and placed her in front of me. I sniffed and instinctively began to lick her off. While I was doing that, I had another labor pain. Tacy looked again. "Oh my, Izzy! Twins!" The second one took a little longer, but she made it just fine. After her mouth and nose were clean, Tacy put her alongside the first one. This one was light

tan with a white strip on her nose and black accents, like me, but her ears were long and hung all the way down, like her father's.

In a few minutes, they had names: the light one became Rachel, and the darker one was Donna Ruth. In only ten minutes they were trying to stand. I got up, too. I noticed I had an udder, and now I knew what it was for! At fifteen minutes of age, they had their first meal of warm milk, and they were clean and dry. Ruckus inched his way closer to observe.

That evening, Tacy put more fresh hay in my corner of the coop. She carried my babies to the coop and put them on the hay. They ate another good meal while I watched their tails wiggle in satisfaction. When they were through, I lay down, and they each found a spot right next to me. I watched as Ruckus looked in at the door before lying down right outside it as guard. The chickens jumped from the ground onto his back, using him as their step up to the door and the wooden floor of the coop. Then they walked by me to pay their regards. Rooster C. clucked softly with approval.

Under the brooder lamp, Rachel and Donna Ruth snuggled up to me and put their heads against my side. Tacy's face smiled in the doorway. I tucked my head gently around my babies. I could hear their tiny heartbeats, and I knew that they were hearing mine, and I knew it beat out the message of love.

*We never know the love of a parent until we become parents ourselves.* – Henry Ward Beecher

## 29. DISAPPEARING CHICKENS

Not long after the kids were born, chickens began to disappear. I counted fewer each evening. Tacy tried keeping us all penned securely and not letting anyone out until she came home from school, but still some disappeared. I would stay near the barn when we were turned out, and Ruckus would watch over our girls and me. The girls would run and bound around. Donna Ruth often lost her footing and wound up on her side or her back on the ground. Rachel was more graceful, but she would bow her neck and rear up to challenge any animal that she met. I enjoyed many hours of watching them grow.

We never went behind the barn, because that is where the chickens disappeared. We would hear a squawk, and Timbra and Dobie would come running to see what was wrong. Tacy would run down with the gun, but by the time they all got there, another chicken was gone. No one knew how to stop the disappearances.

With every chicken that vanished, however, it seemed a new animal would appear. Tacy bought several registered Nubian goats from a friend. She also bought more Spanish goats like me. Then one day, she brought home some animals that were about the same size as a goat, but who were very, very wooly! They had black faces, big, black, dangly ears, and black legs, but they looked puffy because they were covered in wool. Mark asked me one evening, "Izzy, what do you think of the sheep?" I wanted to tell him, "Not much," but I refrained. I thought I should at least give them a chance.

Within a couple of weeks, each new goat had a kid and each new sheep had a lamb alongside it. Ruckus had made friends with the ram, Tom, and they spent their days across the fence from the herd. Each broody hen hatched out another set of peeps, and the new cat had kittens. Spring was in full swing.

Tacy kept the chickens penned up continuously now to prevent their disappearing. But then the lambs began to go! I worried about my babies. One evening Tacy saw a coyote dragging a lamb away and was frantic to know what to do. A solution was too late in coming, however. The next day, Ruckus was killed by a whole pack of coyotes. We mourned him for many days, and, despite his rough character, his funeral was well attended.

*I have known laughter – therefore,*
*I may sorrow with you more tenderly.*
– Theodosia Pickering Garrison

# 30. PECKING ORDER

If there is one thing I learned from being a chicken in my younger days, it is that there must be a pecking order. The strongest or most intelligent must dominate the remainder of the flock or the herd. The order is established usually by age, but sometimes it is challenged by strength. In a flock of chickens, when the boss says to roost, all file in, and in a certain order. That is the order in which the best roosting spots are filled, and the order in which they drink and eat.

After Ruckus was murdered, the goat and sheep herds were merged into the new lot, and we were fed hay until a solution to the coyote problem could be found. Now, this crowded situation was not a good one. I was the oldest goat, and I was older than all the sheep. But there was one registered Nubian doe named Katherine who thought she should be in charge. Now, you know me, that I have never been one to argue...but I knew the procedures here! I knew the danger zones! I had been the first one on this farm. I was the first goat Tacy owned, and I would remain in charge!

The sheep were no problem; they really didn't care who was the leader. They just started toward the hay when someone else did, and started toward the water when someone else wanted a drink. Tom, the ram, took his place at the end of a line of goats.

Katherine picked her time and challenged me when I was at my weakest. I was resting while keeping an eye on Rachel and Donna Ruth near the far fence where they were jumping on a log, then down to the ground, and then back to the top of the log. It was time for them to have their afternoon snack, so I stood and was stretching on two legs when she hit me! She was like a freight train and I, of course, being caught by surprise, went flailing to my side, legs skyward. I stood right up, and was I angry! She was charging again by that time. I braced for the hit. My ears stood straight out, and the hair on my back stood straight up. She hit me head-on, and both of us felt the pain. At least I was ready this time. We both reared up, and our heads fell together at the poll over and over again.

She was beginning to weaken when I noticed that Rachel was not on the log with Donna Ruth. I stopped and called to them and was hit again on the side and knocked down. I went running toward the fence and saw that Rachel had gone through the fence into coyote territory! To onlookers, it appeared that I was running from Katherine, but I couldn't let that bother me, because I must get my babies to safety! I called to Rachel and Donna Ruth, and because they were hungry, they came immediately. I allowed them to nurse while I watched Katherine make her way back to the herd, glancing back at me now and again.

As soon as the babies had nursed, I moved them away from the fence. With their bellies full and the sun shining on them, they collapsed into a heap to take a nap. I headed toward Katherine.

She was standing at the hay feeder in my spot. I bit her tail. She wheeled around at me with her ears raised. I raised my ears and the hair on the middle of my back, then reared up on my hind legs without giving her time to do the same. I lunged toward her, hitting her in the shoulder. Then I did it again and again until she backed off. That time the battle was a fair one. That time, I had won. I walked to the hay feeder and took my spot.

Two days later, Katherine walked up beside me, and I raised my ears. She gently rubbed her head on my side as an apology. I gave her permission to eat beside me. She was, after all, second in the pecking order. No one challenged her, and the rest of the spots were filled by age order. That evening I led the herd, with Katherine second in line, to the barn.

*Good order is the foundation of all good things.*
– Edmund Burke

## 31. THE SOLUTION

Each night the coyotes were coming closer and closer. We feared they would break into the lot. But if they should, we were prepared. Tom would challenge them and hit them to try to drive them back through the fence.

I was lazing in the sun one day, watching Rachel and Donna Ruth establish pecking order with the other kids and lambs. They would run around very fast and then play their version of "king of the hill." The one who could stay on top of the log the longest was the leader. Then they would follow the leader and jump on the backs of various sheep and does until they spotted a new challenger on the log, when the game would begin again.

I heard Tacy's truck pull up. I watched as she unloaded a huge white animal from the back. It was the hairiest animal I had ever seen, and it looked as big as Ruckus had been. It was every bit as big as Tom. As it got closer, I realized that it was a dog!

"Hey, Izzy," Tacy began, "come here and meet Big

Dog Bill Hill." She opened the gate and held him a minute, and I ventured pretty close. The does and sheep were watching me as leader now. I knew that the decision was mine as to whether to accept this new animal or not. Whatever I chose was what the others would choose. I swallowed and approached the new dog.

He was taller than I. His eyes were brown, and the lids were lined with black. He was almost entirely white except for one dark spot on his back. His large, white tail curled up over his back, which made him look even taller. "He's a Great Pyrenees, Izzy. He's a guard dog. He's here to protect you and the herd from the coyotes," explained Tacy.

I thought about that. I approached the animal and sniffed. He sniffed back. The other goats moved in on my signal. He briefly sniffed each one as Tacy led him around. Then she removed his collar and Big Dog Bill Hill ran through the pile of babies, scattering them in every direction. This excited the rest of the herd and woke up the sheep! When he stopped loping, he was at the fence. He threw his head back and barked and howled. Then he went to each corner and did the same.

That night, I kept one eye on my babies and one eye on this strange new dog.

*We love to watch the children's game,*
*their troubles and their joys;*
*For did we not the very same*
*when we were girls and boys?*
– Author Unknown

## 3 2 .   F R E E D O M !

The next day Tacy walked the perimeter of the whole place with Big Dog Bill Hill. Then, after weeks of safety camp in the lot, the gate was opened and we were set free. Babies and mommas alike ran for the green wheat that grew in the open fields. It was wonderful! The green blades were delicious! The babies ran through it, cocking their heads sideways and bolting toward one another. They would get their legs tangled in the grass and fall with their feet ending up skyward...just like someone else I used to know.

All was well...until a coyote showed himself near the fence. A sheep spotted him and called to her babies. He watched the little ones trot to their mother and was starting toward her – when Bill started toward him! The sight of Bill stopped the coyote in his tracks! Bill walked up to him, almost nose to nose, then bared his teeth and growled like thunder. The coyote yelped and literally tucked tail and ran! We did our version of a cheer: we all began eating again.

None of us feared Bill after that. None of us feared coyotes after that. Bill had given us our freedom, expecting nothing from us in return.

*Friendship without self-interest is one of the rare and beautiful things of life.* – James Francis Byrnes

## 33. THE DOMINO EFFECT

Because Ruckus had died, Tacy had to buy a new buck. She picked a very handsome young one named Domino. He was tan-and-white spotted and had really long hair on his legs and shoulders. He was very correct in his conformation. He came in the fall, just in time for breeding season. Tacy took him to a show that winter, and he won it, hands down. He was a registered Nubian. His place was third in the pecking order.

I am not sure what prompted them, but Tacy and Mark decided that a kid of their own would be nice. In February one year, Tacy "dominoed" a healthy baby girl. They named their kid "Sarah". She looked a lot like Tacy, only much smaller. When she was old enough, she would come to the goat pens with Tacy and climb all over us. She would squeal with delight when we sniffed her or gently rubbed our heads on her.

I was always looking out for Sarah as well as for my own babies. Donna Ruth and Rachel were over a year old by the time Sarah began walking, and with Domino I had had a son named Oscar. Sarah could drag Oscar all over the place. Because I had only one kid that year, I had to be milked on one side of my udder every evening. Tacy would put me on the stand and milk into a rubber pail. One evening Sarah insisted she wanted some milk. She had watched as Oscar nursed. She put her hands on the floor of the milk stanchion and opened her mouth below the teat. Tacy squirted milk directly into her mouth – no middle man to pay here! Sarah giggled with delight, clapped her little hands, and made herself ready for more. Again, Tacy squirted my milk into her mouth. This same event was repeated every night for about three weeks. I suppose Sarah was weaned after that, because she quit asking for my milk.

One night while Tacy was milking, I saw Sarah sneak through the gate into the horse pasture. I reached quickly around and pulled Tacy's hair to alert her to the danger, but she misunderstood me. She apologized, thinking she must have squeezed me too hard. So I reached back and pulled again. This time she scolded me. So I had to kick the pail over and toward the front to cause her to turn toward the horses.

Then she saw Sarah and ran to get her, but too late! Sarah had grabbed the leg of a horse, and he had taken off running. She wasn't hurt too badly, but she was crying because it had scared her. After that, Tacy had Sarah hold the milk pail – and she fixed the gate! Of course, she thanked me, too. Just to make certain Sarah did not get through the gate again, Katherine joined me in her care, placing herself between Sarah and the fence. If Sarah started toward the gate, Katherine made a beeline to bump her gently in the other direction.

Another time, Sarah was playing on a log, tapping it with a rock, and she stirred up a nest of fire ants. I saw them swarming on her, so I ran and knocked her from the log and rubbed her leg with my head until Tacy could get there.

Sarah always rubbed on me and dug her fingers into my hair. How good it felt when her little fingers scratched deeply into my fur. Sometimes, when Sarah grew tired, I would position myself behind her so she could lean against me as though I were a solid wall, putting her elbows on top of my back and propping her foot on my knee. When she would yawn and her head would bob, I would stop chewing my cud for a minute and wiggle just enough to keep her awake until Tacy was ready to go to the house. I was always thankful that Tacy and Mark "dominoed" with Sarah.

*Love starts when another person's needs*
*become more important than your own.*
– Anna Cummins

## 34. THE MIGHTY OAK

When Sarah was about four, and I had had kids for the fourth time, we moved into town in Woodson. Our pasture there had something really special...TREES! Not just old mesquite trees, or mulberry trees, or hackberry trees, but oak trees! And they were huge oak trees!

The sheep had been sold before we moved to town, but all of the goats made the move. We goats cleaned up briars and small weeds and those branches that hung low enough for us to reach. We climbed those trees, and at any given time, goats

could be seen asleep in a tree, legs dangling down. It was while we lived among the mighty oaks that our prayers were answered: the drought ended.

Katherine and I, by then, had become friends. A friend of Tacy's offered to breed her to a different buck, so Tacy drove Katherine to her friend's place. The friend was to call Tacy and let her know when Katherine was ready for home. When the friend did call, she said she had good and bad news. The good news was that Katherine was bred. The bad news was that she had been in an accident. Her front left leg was broken and her shoulder crushed. Tacy hurried away to get Katherine.

She brought her home and put her under the mighty oak. Katherine couldn't get up or down. Her leg caused her great pain. Tacy made a call to a veterinarian and arranged to have her seen. Katherine had to have her leg amputated, but the day she came home, she was better. She lay under the oak, and I brought her branches from which to eat the leaves. When she had eaten them all, she got up on her own and followed me, and we found some other leaves.

Now, I may have been the leader in the pecking order, but Katherine is the one who will be remembered for years. You see, registered herds need a herd name, and Katherine, being three-legged now, became our mascot, and Tripod Nubians became our herd name. All the babies from the herd would carry the name "Tripod" for years to come. Katherine had made her mark. Her daughters would go on to win many shows and her sons to have many daughters. And I would be remembered as her friend.

Our days with the mighty oaks were wonderful. We believed this would be a place to stay forever, but we were wrong....

*Arrange whatever pieces come your way.*
– Virginia Woolf

## 35. PECOS, TEXAS

In 1989 we moved to Pecos, Texas. Well, ten of us moved. I went, as did Tripod Katherine, Domino, Donna Ruth, Rachel, and five other registered does. The others were sold. Five members of my original flock also made the trip, but Rooster C. was no longer a part of our lives. He had been buried beneath the mighty oak. Timbra came along and so did Big Dog Bill Hill, but Dobie had gone to the great hunting ground in the sky. Sarah, Mark, and Tacy all made the move.

Pecos was 120 degrees on a good day in the summer. It was a dry heat, but that doesn't mean much besides "it was hot." We lived in Pecos when my successor was born. It was the first spring we were there. Katherine had trouble with her triplets that year. She had one huge black doe kid that Tacy had to help deliver. They named her Mozelle, and she was ornery! She ate from Katherine, but if any other doe stood still long enough, she would butt the rightful kids off and steal the milk for herself!

She fought the other kids off the feeder. She guarded the water trough and did not allow anyone else to drink. Katherine could not control her.

I had two buck kids that year. They were very handsome. I loved them very much, but I had learned over the years that the buck kids had to be sold; only the does could stay. It was good to see Rachel and Donna Ruth in the herd and to know that Ruckus's and my legacy would live on. I wished for a doe kid with Domino, but it was not to be. People drove for long distances to buy his kids. Because I was not registered, my kids could not be registered either, and my boys were sold for show purposes. The following winter, when they were almost yearlings, my boys won the county stock shows where they lived, and both placed at the livestock exposition in Fort Worth. I was glad when Tacy shared the news with me. She was good about that. She always talked to me believing I would understand – and I did.

Mozelle first challenged me for position during her yearling season. I easily put her in her place, but Katherine was appalled and shocked that her child would do such a thing. I told her not to worry, that there was a purpose for Mozelle's boldness.

*No joy in nature is so sublimely affecting as the*
*joy of a mother at the good fortune of her child.*
– Jean Paul Richter

## 36. THE PACIFIER

Tacy had a boy that year. His name was Drew, but all the cowboys called him "Smiley." He kept a pacifier in his mouth most of the time. When someone would talk to him, he would pluck it out and grin really big and then fasten it back in.

He was eleven months old when he started walking around in the goat pen. He would toddle here and there and pet us and offer us his pacifier. Of course, Mozelle was the only one who took it! When she did, I was there; I bit her ear and made her drop it. Tacy picked it up and walked to the water trough where she dipped it in to wash it off. Then she gave it back to Smiley Drew.

Now, little Smiley Drew liked how cool that pacifier felt after it came out of the water trough. Each evening while Tacy milked, he would stand and dip his pacifier in the trough and then suck on it some more. I would stand there and guard him from the other goats while I chewed my cud.

One night when I wasn't feeling too well, one of the smaller does went to see what Smiley Drew was doing. He dipped his pacifier in the water and, remembering what Mozelle had done, he didn't offer it to the little doe, but just stuck his hand out to her instead. She licked it a little, because he was always eating some kind of candy and the scent was on his hand. Well, Mozelle was watching all of this. She moseyed over to little Smiley Drew and waited for her turn to lick his hand.

He dipped his pacifier and put out his hand. Mozelle looked right at me and then at his hand. Then she grabbed his hand and began chewing it in her grinders! I jumped up, ran at her, and hit her sideways into the fence. I knocked the breath out of her. (I didn't dare let on that it hurt me, too.) Tacy had seen the whole thing, but she just couldn't get there in time. She thanked me for watching little Drew and then took him inside the house to doctor his hand.

*You have to count on living every single day in a way*
*you believe will make you feel good about your life*
*– so that if it were over tomorrow,*
*you'd be content with yourself.*
*– Jane Seymour*

## 37. END OF THE LINE

I regarded Mozelle in disgust. She was ruining the good name of goats! I looked at Katherine standing beside her, and at the other goats around her. I turned away from Mozelle, and everyone else followed. There she stood, alone in the pen. For the next few days, we all gave her the cold shoulder. She was demoted to the end of the pecking order. Even Big Dog Bill Hill ignored her.

She would come to the feed trough, and we would all walk away. We would be watering and she would walk up, and we would all move away to lie down. Mozelle would come to lie down in the herd, and we would get up and move to a new location. It sounds harsh, but it softened her.

Her eyes met mine one day, pleading for a friend. I moved down and let her eat with me. The others saw that I had allowed her in, and gradually they allowed her to come back into their good graces. She started being watchful that everyone else was tended to before she herself began to eat. Mozelle was still at the end of the line in the pecking order, but she was working her way up.

I watched one day as she put herself between a horse and little Smiley Drew when she thought he might be in danger. I watched as she allowed others to eat before she did. I watched as she lay with her mother, Katherine, and allowed Katherine to brace her body against her to relieve the weight on her tired, double-duty leg. One day, Mozelle gathered up all the babies right before a surprise dust storm hit, and another time she made certain that Katherine got up and headed inside before a hailstorm came through. Yes, there was a purpose for Mozelle's boldness, and soon it would be served.

*Begin each day with friendly thoughts,*
*and as the day goes on, keep friendly, loving,*
*good, and kind, just as you were at dawn.*
– Frank B. Whitney

## 38. REST IN PECOS

I didn't have a kid this spring. I watched the other mothers with their kids. I watched my daughters and my grandchildren. It is great fun to watch them discover the world. Now, I watch Tacy as she grows older, and I watch her kids grow up, too. They are happy; she is raising them like she raised me. Timbra passes the time with me. She watches over me. Bill stops by and throws his head back and

howls. I chew my cud. The members of my herd take turns resting beside me. Tacy comes out every evening and helps me up and pets me and rubs my swollen knees. She brings me raisins.

I am a goat who started out as a chicken. I have been afraid, and I have been brave. I have learned, and I have discovered. I was allowed to be curious. I have been loved. I have known many heartbeats, and though mine slows now, I know it lives on through my children and my teaching. I am at rest in Pecos.

*Endeavor to live your life so that if you died today, even the undertaker would be sorry.* – Mark Twain

# 39. GOOD-BYE
## By Mozelle

I am not the writer or storyteller that Izzy was. Her funeral was today. I led the way. My mother followed. Izzy's family was next. Domino was the last goat. Timbra, Bill, Smiley Drew, Sarah, and Mark were there. Tacy was the last to say good-bye. We stood with great respect and watched as she cried. But a goat must go on, and so I led my herd away, with Izzy's blessing. The guidance that Izzy offered will be the basis of my leadership, and my boldness will serve a purpose.

*True friends have no solitary joy or sorrow.*
– William Ellery Channing

*Life, for all its agonies of despair, loss and guilt,*
*is exciting and beautiful, full of liking and love; at times*
*a poem and a high adventure, at times noble and at*
*times very gay; and whatever is to come after it –*
*we shall not have this life again.*
– Rose Macaulay

# FACT FINDER AND GOAT GLOSSARY

## DEFINITIONS AND TERMS TO UNDERSTAND

**Doe** a female goat that has borne a kid

**Kid** a baby goat

**Doe kid** a female baby goat

**Buck kid** a male baby goat

**Buck** a male goat

**Wattles** the little "hangy-down" things under the jaw of some goats; used in nature as a protection measure to confuse predators

**Udder** the milk gland on a goat

**Teat** the part of the milk gland where baby goats nurse

**Poll** the top of a goat's head

**Hoof** the foot of a goat, which is cloven, or split into two halves. The hoof consists of the hard outer covering on the two halves, the floor or face that touches the ground, and all the inner gelatin and bones.

**Cloven hoof** a hoof made of two toes, as in goats, sheep, deer, and cattle

**Horn Buttons** hard buds on the polls of young goats where horns are beginning to grow

**Conformation** the structure, shape, and form of an animal

**Dish Face** Facial characteristic found in Alpines, Saanens, Toggenburgs, Oberhaslis, Spanish goats and some crosses in which the face, if viewed from the side, "scoops" slightly from the brow (just above the eyes) to the muzzle. It is acceptable, but a straight noseline is more desirable.

**Roman Nose** Breed characteristic of Nubians and Boers in which the face, when viewed from the side, looks like the back of a bow (bow and arrow) and is bowed out from the brow to the muzzle.

**Pendulous Ears** ears that hang downward and extend below the jawline 1 to 2 inches. Breed requirement for Nubians, Boers, and some crosses.

**Shear** to trim the hair on a goat

**Clip hooves** to trim the "toenails" of a goat

**Disbud** to remove the horns of a goat with a heated iron while the goat is young

**Castrate** to remove the testicles from a male goat

**Purebred** a goat whose parents are of the same registered breed and can therefore be registered

**Recorded Grade** a dairy goat that has only one registered parent from any of the registered breeds

**Cross** any goat whose parents are each from a different breed

**Meat goat** a goat primarily raised to be sold for butchering; more heavily muscled than a dairy goat

**Dairy goat** any goat raised to produce milk

**Hair goat** any goat raised to be shorn each year for hair


## PRODUCTS THAT GOATS GIVE US

**Mohair** – When hair is sheared, or cut, from goats it is called *mohair*. Mohair is cleaned, dried, and sorted by quality. It is "carded" (passed through brushes with thousands of tiny teeth) to straighten and untangle it. Then it is twisted into a "sliver" (a continuous string) and finally spun into yarn. Cashmere is an extremely soft and expensive type of mohair.

**Milk** – Goat's milk is more easily digested than cow's milk and is recommended for infants and people who have difficulty with cow's milk. The curd is much smaller and more digestible, and it is naturally homogenized. Contrary to popular opinion, goat's milk is not naturally bad tasting; however, if it is not handled properly and cooled quickly, it can take on odors from its surroundings.

**Cheese** – Goat's milk is used to make cheeses such as Rocamadour, Chevre, and feta.

**Soap** – Some chemists call goat's milk "nature's liposome" because it is easily absorbed into the skin. Soap made from goat's milk restores moisture, protein, minerals and vitamins to the skin.

**Meat** – Goat meat, called *chevon*, is similar to veal or venison. It can be prepared in the same ways as any other meat. Its cholesterol level is comparable to thst of chicken. It is a staple in the Middle East, Central America, Italy, Greece, Turkey, Asia, and Africa and is rapidly gaining popularity in America.

**Hide** – In times past, goat hide was used for water and wine bottles in both traveling and in transporting wine for sale. It was also used to produce parchment, the most common writing material in Europe until the invention of the printing press. Today, goat skin is still used today to make gloves, boots, and other products that require a soft leather.

## HEIFER INTERNATIONAL

• A program in which farm animals are contributed to families in third-world countries to help support the population. Goats are the most commonly contributed animals because they are easy to care for, require only small acreage, and are an inexpensive source of milk and meat.

## HEALTH FACTS

• Goats are ruminants, which means they have more than one stomach. (Other ruminant animals include cattle, sheep, deer, and camels.) As ruminants, goats chew "cud" – the grass they have eaten during grazing that has had moisture extracted, has been regurgitated (brought back into the mouth), and is chewed again to maximize the nutrients taken in. The cud is swallowed again and then passes through all four stomachs and into the small intestine.

• Goats have a full set of upper and lower grinding teeth in the back of their jaws, but only eight teeth in the front of their mouths. All eight of these teeth are on the lower jaw. Goats have no teeth on the upper part of their mouths in front.

• A goat's normal body temperature is 102-103°F. If you think your goat is sick, start by taking its temperature.

• If a goat doesn't eat at feeding time, it is probably sick.

• If a goat's tail is down and stays down, it might be sick.

• If a goat grinds its teeth, it might be sick.

• Goats can carry internal parasites and should be dewormed at least every two months.

• Another type of internal parasite is Coccidia, and most goat feed is now medicated to control this deadly infestation.

• Goats need their "kidhood" vaccines, just as humans do. Vaccinations for enterotoxemia and tetanus are most common.

• Goats need shelter from the rain and wind to prevent respiratory problems. Barns must be well ventilated and dry.

• Sometimes goats get soremouth, which causes ugly and painful sores on their lips. It is contagious to other goats. It takes about three weeks for soremouth to run its course, but once the goat is over the disease, it should have lifetime immunity. Once the disease is on a farm, it will be in the soil permanently and will infect new animals when conditions become favorable.

## REPRODUCTION

• In some warm climates, goats can breed all year, but in most of the United States, they breed in late spring, summer, and fall.

• Goats have a gestation period of about 151 days. That is how long it takes for the fetus to form, develop, and grow, and finally, to be born.

• Goats are born as twins most often, although triplets and quadruplets are not uncommon.

• The birthing process is called *kidding.*

• Does come into milk, or *freshen,* at kidding time, producing from 1,500 – 4,000 pounds of milk in the next 305 days. The time they are in milk is known as *lactation.*

• Within minutes of birth, the kids are on their feet and nursing. They begin to travel around the lot or pasture by the third day of their lives.

## GOAT NUTRITION

• Goats are very picky eaters. They don't eat tin cans or paper. They merely pick these items up to "feel" them, since they don't have fingers. If feed is soiled in any way, goats will not eat it.

• Goats are browsers. This means they prefer to eat anything eye-level or above. They will graze when browsing is not available.

• Goats need to eat at least two times per day, although they prefer to eat three times, like humans.

• An adult goat can maintain itself on two to four pounds of feed per day, but a goat that is nursing kids may need from four to eight pounds of feed per day. Goats need roughage (grazing, browsing, or hay) in addition to feed.

• A good feed should contain at least 16% protein.

• Pelleted feed has been found to be best for goats,

as they are quite picky when it comes to eating and will pick out the "good stuff" if it is fed in a mixed ration.

• Oats are a good feed for goats.

• Fresh water is important on a daily basis.


# COMMON BREEDS OF GOATS

## DAIRY BREEDS

LARGE DAIRY BREEDS (Females mature at 150 pounds; males at 250-300 pounds)

**Alpine** a dairy goat with erect ears and a dished face; specific color patterns

**Nubian** a dairy goat with long pendulous ears and a Roman nose; any color

**Toggenburg** a dairy goat with erect ears and a dished face, color being light to dark tan with white feet, underline and facial accents

**Saanen** a dairy goat with erect ears and a dished face; solid white

**Oberhasli** a dairy goat with erect ears and a dished face; black and tan

**LaMancha** a dairy goat with a dished face and little or no external ears; any color

MINIATURE DAIRY BREED (Both males and females mature at about 50 pounds)

**Nigerian Dwarf** a dairy goat with erect ears and a dished face; often incorrectly referred to as a "pygmy" goat; usually black or gray, but can be any color

## MEAT BREEDS

**Boer** a meat goat with the dominant color pattern of white with a reddish-colored head

**American Meat Goat** relatively new breed that can be any color. The goats should have that structural correctness that contributes to muscle volume and survivability.

**Kiko** In New Zealand, the word *kiko* means *meat*. Domestic milk goats there escaped into the wild and, through natural selection, evolved into the hardy Kiko. They are larger framed than other breeds of goats and have high conversion rates of roughage eaten to weight gained. They produce a lean carcass.

**Spanish Goats** The first breed recognized in Texas. Developed from the LaMancha goat, a goat suitable for both milk and meat production, which was brought to the New World by Spanish missionaries. The Spanish Goat is used for brush control and meat production.

## DAIRY BREED HISTORY

**LaMancha** – Spanish missionaries brought the LaMancha goat with them to the New World, for it was a breed suitable for milk and for meat production. LaManchas, known for their short, gopher-like ears, appeared at the Paris World's Fair in 1904 and were accepted as a breed for registry in 1958.

**Alpine** – Alpines can survive on steep mountains or in arid (dry) regions. They are raised for milk production. They have unique personalities, which made the breed a good choice for voyages across the ocean in an age of exploration. Alpines are thought to have been brought to America on the Mayflower.

**Saanen** – The Saanen dairy goat originated in Switzerland and was first imported into the United States in 1904, to improve common American goats through cross-breeding.

## HAIR BREEDS

**Angora** a hair goat that is white in color and is smaller than the Cashmere breed

**Cashmere** a hair goat with extremely soft, curly white hair

## SHOWING

• Almost every goat association has its own sanctioned shows for its breed, in which goats must conform to rigid breed standards. To be eligible for showing, goats must usually be registered. Registered goats bring a higher price and are sold for production purposes.

• There are also market shows, where animals are exhibited to display their meat characteristics. The Boer goat and crosses derived from it are most commonly shown at these shows, and animals competing there are sold for slaughter.

## DID YOU KNOW

• Mountain Goats are not true goats, but belong to the group *Rupricaprini,* which includes the antelope. They live in mountains above the timberline and eat lichens, moss, shrubs, and grass.

• Goats were the first animals domesticated by man over 12,000 years ago.

• Because of goats' docility, throughout history, most goatherds have been children.

• In 1630, goats were listed as one of the most valuable assets of the farmers in the Jamestown Colony.

• The 1904 World's Fair in St. Louis, Missouri, held the first dairy-goat show in America.

• The word *caprine* is to goats as *canine* is to dogs, *feline* is to cast, or *equine* is to the horse.

• In Scandinavia, it is traditional to have a straw goat under the Christmas tree.

• Goat races have been held in the Caribbean Islands since 1925.

• Race-horse trainers used to stable goats with horses because they believed the goats would keep excitable thoroughbreds calm.

## GOAT SAYINGS

• "Get your goat" – to annoy someone
• "Scapegoat" – someone who is blamed or punished for another person's mistake
• "Just kidding" – joking or teasing
• "Handle with kid gloves" – treating a person or problem with great sensitivity

## GOATS IN HISTORY AND FOLKLORE

• The *Julbukk* in Swedish and Norwegian lore is otherwise known as the "Yule goat." He carries the Yule elf, *Jultomte,* on his back to deliver presents during the Christmastime.

• In Norse mythology, the chariot of Thor was drawn by the goats Tanngnjostr and Tanngrisnr.

• In Greek and Roman mythology, Pan was the god of flocks and shepherds. He is depicted as having the horns and lower body of a goat with the upper body of a man, a creature known as a *satyr*. He is often pictured playing panpipes made from reeds.


## GOAT STORIES

• *The Goatherd and the Wild Goats* is one of *Aesop's Fables*.

• *The Goat and the Dog: A Balinese Folktale* conjectures that the relationship between dogs and goats was established when the dog traded his horns for the goat's long tail.

• *Zlateh the Goat and Other Stories* by Isaac B. Singer and illustrated by Maurice Sendak, was a 1967 Newbery Honor Book.

• *The Three Billy Goats Gruff* is a much loved Norwegian fairy tale in which three goats trick a troll and are able to cross his bridge.

# GOATS IN ART

- *The Scapegoat* by William Holman Hunt
- *Man with Goat* by Pablo Picasso
- *She-Goat, a sculpture* by Pablo Picasso
- *Five Amorini Playing with a Goat* by Agostini Carracci
- *Esmeralda Teaching the Goat to Spell Her Lover's Name* and *Just for Kids,* two sculptures by Robin Laws

# SOURCES AND USEFUL WEBSITES

http://www.unitedcaprinenews.com/index.shtml

American Dairy Goat Association: http://adga.org

American Goat Society: http://americangoatsociety.com

American Boer Goat Association: http://abga.org/

United Caprine News

December 2005 <http://www.unitedstreaming.com/>.

Ruminant Animals. United Learning. 2004. unitedstreaming. 8

December 2005 <http://www.unitedstreaming.com/>

http://www.meatgoats.com/

http://www.emeraldfarm.com/soapfactory/index.htm

http://amnh.org/exhibitions/dioramas/goat/

http://www.lamanchas.com/lm-history.htm

http://en.wikipedia.org/wiki/Goat

http://www.alpinesinternationalclub.com/history_alphist.htm

http://www.karlschatz.com/yearofthegoat/primer.shtml  great
place to see pictures.

http://www.webworksltd.com/webpub/goats/faintinggoat.html

http://rebelridge.com/history.htm

# PARTS OF A GOAT

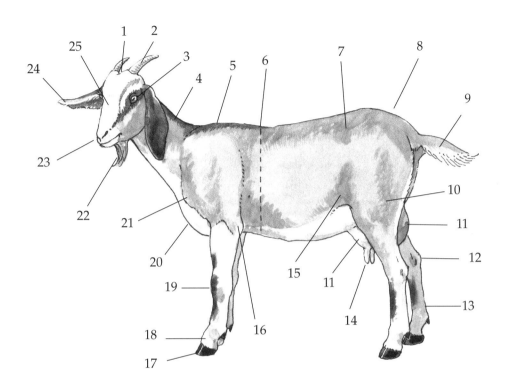

| | | |
|---|---|---|
| 1. Poll | 10. Thigh | 19. Knee |
| 2. Horn | 11. Udder | 20. Brisket |
| 3. Eye | 12. Hock | 21. Point of |
| 4. Neck | 13. Leg | shoulder |
| 5. Withers | 14. Teat | 22. Beard |
| 6. Heart girth | 15. Flank | 23. Muzzle |
| 7. Hip bone | 16. Elbow | 24. Ear |
| 8. Rump | 17. Hoof | 25. Bridge of |
| 9. Tail | 18. Pastern | nose |